Celadon

✴ A Strange Space™ Novel ✴

Katie Silverwings

Memphis, TN

PepTalk Productions, LLC

Publisher's Cataloging-in-Publication Data
provided by Five Rainbows Cataloging Services

Names: Silverwings, Katie, 1991- author.
Title: Celadon : a strange space novel / Katie Silverwings
Description: Memphis, TN : PepTalk Productions, 2024. | Series:
    Strange space adventures, bk. 2.
Identifiers: LCCN 2024917955 (print) | ISBN 978-1-959922-26-1
    (paperback) | ISBN 978-1-959922-27-8 (hardcover) | ISBN 978-1-
    959922-28-5 (ebook) | ISBN 978-1-959922-29-2 (audiobook)
Subjects: LCSH: Extraterrestrial beings--Fiction. | Family--Fiction.
    | Friendship--Fiction. | Outer space--Fiction. | Science fiction. |
    Illustrated works. | BISAC: FICTION / Science Fiction / Alien
    Contact. | FICTION / Friendship. | GSAFD: Science fiction.
Classification: LCC PS3619.I58 Ce 2024 (print) | LCC PS3619.I58
    (ebook) | DDC 813/.6--dc23.

Second Edition

Published by PepTalk Productions, LLC 2024
Memphis, Tennessee, USA
www.PepTalkProductionsLLC.com

To the family I was born to and the family I've chosen.
All of you are precious pieces of my story.

Books by Katie Silverwings

FEATHERED FRIENDSHIP
✶ A Strange Space™ Novella ✶

CELADON
✶ A Strange Space™ Novel ✶

HOW OCEAN MERLANI STOLE THEIR NAVIGATOR
✶ A Strange Space™ Novel ✶

WARMTH AND DARKNESS
✶ A Strange Space™ Novella ✶

THE GARDEN IN THE DARKNESS
✶ A Strange Space™ Novel ✶

TALES OF THE NAVIGATORS: VOLUME 1
✶ Strange Space™ Short Stories ✶

ON THE SUBJECT OF KITTENS AND MITTENS
✶ A Strange Space™ Novella ✶

The printing of this edition of *Celadon* was made possible through the generous support of the members of the Strange Space Fan Club, including:

Astral Navigator

Sharon T. Hinton

Space Adventurer (1 Year)

Tabitha

Thank you so much to all of my Fan Club members and supporters! I couldn't do this without you.

To find out more about the Strange Space Fan Club and join for free, visit:

www.KatieSilverwings.com/Fan-Club

Celadon: A Strange Space™ Novel received the 2023 Richard Wright Literary Award for Best Adult Fantasy/ Science Fiction from the Memphis Public Libraries.

Characters Appearing in this Story

The following list of characters is divided by species and arranged in order of their appearance in the narrative. Only characters with significant "speaking roles" have been detailed here. All others present are listed as a group for the reader's reference; characters who are mentioned but do not appear are not included.

Humans

Admiral Jennifer Marvin
She/her. Also known as "Jenny". Head of the Sol Coalition Defense Fleet.

Ensign Hsu Li
He/him. Personal Assistant to **Admiral Jennifer Marvin.**

Monica Malarius
She/her. Retired Astral Navigator. Counterpart to **Indigo Taivin.**

Joseph St. Claire
He/him. Lead Astral Navigator, ESS *Deinocheirus.* Counterpart to **Elder Caeruleus Altarin.**

Rebecca Montgomery
She/Her. Lead Astral Navigator, LSS *Caleana Major.* Counterpart to Elder Azul.

Other Humans Appearing
Mx. Finch Carlyle

Florivans

ELDER CELADON TOREVAL

They/them. Also known as "Donnie". Youngest of the Florivan Council of Elders. Parent of **Jade Ilmi, Teal Iralee, Turquoise Inayan** and **Lapis Taldee**. Child of **Elder Lazurite Ylmri**. Heart's-child of **the Eldest**.

JADE ILMI

They/them. A survivor-smallest kitten. Star-Keeper in training. Littermate of **Teal Iralee** and **Turquoise Inayan**. Child of **Elder Celadon**.

LAPIS TALDEE

They/them. Sibling of **Jade Ilmi**. Child of **Elder Celadon.**

TEAL IRALEE AND TURQUOISE INAYAN

They/them. (Deceased.) Members of the Lone Star Ranger Corps. Children of **Elder Celadon**. Littermates of **Jade Ilmi**.

INDIGO TAIVIN

They/them. Also known as "Indi". Retired Quantum Space Drive Engineer, baker. Eldest sibling of Elder Woad. Counterpart to **Monica Malarius**.

NAVY IRLEEIM

They/them. Resident Psychologist, Teegarden Shipyards. Child of Elder Bughaw.

THE ELDEST

They/them. Eldest of the Florivan Council of Elders. Parent of **Ocean Marbree, River Myrval, Sky Laryven** and **Stream Liret**. Parental figure and mentor to **Elder Celadon**. Eldest sibling of **Elder Caeruleus**.

Elder Caeruleus Altarin

They/them. Also known as "Cae". Lead Quantum Space Drive Engineer, ESS *Deinocheirus*. Youngest sibling of **the Eldest**. Mentor to **Ocean Marbree** and **River Myrval**. Counterpart to **Joseph St. Claire**.

Ocean Marbree

They/them. Apprentice to **Elder Caeruleus**. Child of **the Eldest**. Littermate of **River Myrval** and sibling of **Sky Laryven** and **Stream Liret**.

River Myrval

They/them. A survivor-smallest kitten. Apprentice to **Elder Caeruleus**. Child of **the Eldest**. Littermate of **Ocean Marbree** and sibling of **Sky Laryven** and **Stream Liret**.

Sky Laryven

They/them. Secondary Quantum Space Drive Engineer, ESS *Cetorhinus*. Child of **the Eldest**. Littermate of **Stream Liret**. Heart's-littermate of **Elder Celadon**. Counterpart to Deirdre Roberts.

Myrie (and Littermates)

They/them. The kittens of **Elder Lazurite's** youngest litter.

Other Florivans Appearing

A geologist of Elder Azul's household, Elder Kyanite, Elder Celeste, Elder Azul, the Florivan Council of Elders, the Siblings of Celadon Toreval, the Story-Keepers

CONTENTS

CONTENTS

Celadon

★ A Strange Space™ Novel ★

KATIE SILVERWINGS

Part 1: The Youngest and The Ensign

THERE ARE FEW PLACES BETTER FOR SILENTLY observing a conversation without being noticed than a tangle of rafters and support beams high above the balcony where the speakers are standing.

In Celadon Toreval's mind, their people's Council House must have been designed with such purposes in mind—not that any of the other Elders would ever admit to climbing up into the rafters themselves at all. That sort of behavior is expected of kittens, naturally, but an *Elder* is expected to carry themself with a certain amount of dignity.

Dignity or not, Toreval spends a lot of their time in the Council House rafters, even when they *don't* have a pair of interesting aliens to listen to. It's part of their role to make themself aware of all things going on, after all—and the Eldest doesn't seem to mind having them drop down from above when their opinion is actually called for. Toreval has never really cared what any of the others think, if they're honest.

This present bit of listening is on Toreval's own account, though, rather than the Council's. They've placed themself just close enough that their keen catlike ears can swivel and focus on the voices of the two aliens, but still far away enough that one of the speakers would have to look up at precisely the right angle and location to see them at all. Their long prehensile tail curls around the beam they're sitting on for stability, while their four hands lightly anchor them to the support beams. They have both legs loosely crossed, their lightweight sandals long since removed and tucked neatly into the folds of their sash for the sake of greater ease in climbing. The pale greenish-blue of their silver-striped skin and the amber layers of their robes disappear into the rich browns of the wood around them and the deep shadows cast by the Council House roof.

The people Toreval is observing are too caught up in their conversation to consider looking up and seeing the Florivan Elder whose three golden eyes peer out of the shadows in the rafters, of course. The human Admiral and her young assistant have a lot to talk about, now that they've left the Council chamber and are waiting to be told where their guest quarters will be and if the Florivan Council of Elders has anything else to say to them today.

"I'm telling you, Admiral," says a voice which Toreval assumes must belong to the young man who'd stood silently by the Admiral's side throughout her speech to the Council, with a light sigh of resignation coloring his smoothly accented words, "there's no way this plan of yours is going to work."

"Oh?" asks the Admiral, in much the same curious but parental tone Toreval themself often uses when their kittens are struggling to understand something. "And why do you think that, Ensign?"

"They're a species of *pacifists*, Ma'am," the Ensign replies pointedly. "Their Council is never going to willingly throw in with us in the middle of a war."

"We're not asking them to fight."

"No, but after what happened to your Rangers—"

"—My Rangers are why we are *here*, Ensign."

In the silence that follows, Toreval quietly shifts position to a perch where they may more closely watch the body language of the two humans. It's a good distraction from the stab of regret and grief that the Admiral's words have sparked in the back of their thoughts.

Admiral Marvin herself is standing close to the curtained archway between the balcony and the waiting chamber inside, her single pair of arms crossed over her chest. A tall russet-skinned woman with all her light brown curls pulled back into a bun and held with a pair of long brass hairpins, in general bearing and attitude she strikes Toreval as being very like some of the senior Elders they've trained under: driven, confident, and with an air of genuine concern for the people under her command.

The Admiral's young assistant, meanwhile, is halfway leaning against the balcony railing now, looking out at the courtyard below. A light breeze catches the long leaf-black hair he's wearing up in a high ponytail, making it shift and shimmer against his tawny-pale skin and the green of his Defense Fleet uniform. He was so quiet and politely attentive during the proceedings earlier that Toreval has been unable to make any assessments of his character, aside from the loyalty he obviously has towards the Admiral. His posture now indicates that he's quite comfortable with the woman he serves, enough that he clearly does not fear to speak honestly to her.

"I just don't think they'll agree to help us if it means abandoning their customs."

"Your lack of faith is noted, Ensign." The Admiral joins the younger human at the railing and sets a hand on his shoulder briefly. "But I have no time for pessimism when this may be our only hope to survive."

"...Yes, Ma'am."

"Now," the Admiral says, her tone shifting to something almost affectionately parental, "why don't you go get to know the locals while I wait for word about our accommodations?"

"Ma'am?" The Ensign seems startled by the request.

"You're my assistant, aren't you? I'm relying on your observational skills while we're here. Go explore the city a bit and see if you can learn anything that will help our cause." She stifles a chuckle. "Besides, we're supposed to look like we're on leave, and we'll likely be here a while yet. It wouldn't do to keep you cooped up here and have folks wonder what official business we might really be here for."

"But Admiral—"

"—Do I need to make that an *order*, Ensign?"

The Ensign shakes his head reluctantly, then gives her a small salute. "You don't, Ma'am."

"Good. Have fun—see if you can find us somewhere interesting to have dinner, while you're at it."

"Yes, Admiral."

Toreval watches from their perch high in the rafters as the Ensign walks away. They would have liked to hear the rest of the younger human's thoughts, but that can wait. They will make a chance to talk to him later.

They have other business to attend to first.

"Your Ensign may be right, you know."

The Admiral looks up to them with much the same expression their parent usually wears when they see Toreval up in the rafters: something halfway between disapproving and amused. "I was unaware that *eavesdropping* was one of your people's habits, Youngest."

Toreval drops down onto the balcony railing beside the Admiral. The amber silks of their robes catch the breeze nicely as they take a comfortable position on one corner of the railing and steady themself with their long, tufted prehensile tail and lower pair of hands. This meeting is far different in tone than the formal introduction the two of them had an hour ago when she first stood before the Eldest and the other members of the Council who are present today. They're amused, though, that she's still deferring to their proper title. They wonder if that's out of respect, or if she's simply not remembered their public name out of the eighteen Elders she met earlier.

"I wanted to speak to you."

The Admiral raises an eyebrow. "On behalf of the Council?"

"On my own account." Toreval dips their head lightly.

"I see... I would have thought you'd all still be in there deliberating."

"The final decision regarding your proposal won't be made until the rest of the Elders arrive." Toreval shrugs, twitching one of their ears. "Until then, *I* don't care to waste time arguing about it."

"What did you want to say to me, then?"

Toreval looks out towards the city. They can see the Ensign crossing the courtyard now, one lone human figure among the blue and silver bustle of their people. They watch him as he turns and looks towards the upper levels of the Council House, one hand shielding his eyes from the smaller sun which is doubtless cresting its domes at this hour. After a few moments, he lowers his hand and continues walking, disappearing down one of the side streets that leads towards the River which cuts through the heart of their home.

"Why are you here, Admiral?" Toreval asks at last.

"You heard my case already, Youngest." The Admiral leans against the railing and joins them in gazing out over the city. "I'm here to get permission to recruit volunteers from your people for the Fleet."

"So you said. What I want to know is *why*."

"We don't stand a chance of surviving this war against the Novans without your technology—"

"—You already have our technology on your interstellar vessels." Toreval gives her a knowing look with their third eye, keeping the lower two directed towards the courtyard.

"*Civilian* vessels, yes, or *Ranger* ones. Never the Defense Fleet's."

"True."

"If we could use the Drive without you—or if anyone *else* was willing or able to share their post-light tech—I wouldn't be here. I'd have the whole Fleet outfitted and flying instead of sitting around on the edges of all of our systems waiting to be attacked."

"That is not by our design, Admiral."

"I know."

Toreval is silent for a few moments, watching the courtyard below. They're well aware of the fact that human ships on their own are limited to relatively slow-moving solar sail flight, and that it's only thanks to their people's gift of the so-called 'Quantum Space Drive' that interstellar journeys are possible for them in weeks or months rather than decades. Likewise, they're *personally* familiar with the role a Florivan plays as the member of such a starship's crew who runs the Drive and safely jumps the ship back and forth through the veil between 'Normal' space and the dimension their people know as the Strange with the help of their human Navigator counterpart.

"We've been trying to integrate with your species for a century now," Toreval says at last. "Do you know how many times we've been approached by those who would adapt our technology for warfare, even before our peoples met?"

"No, although I can imagine... But the present situation is different."

"Is it?"

"The Novans know that your people exist now."

Toreval turns all three of their eyes back to the human. "What do you mean by that, Admiral Marvin?"

The Admiral holds eye contact with them for a few moments, and then lets out a half sigh and looks away, back towards the domes of the city and the purple-black treetops beyond.

"Just after we got pulled into the war," she says, folding her hands together, "I was approached by two Ranger pairs who volunteered to help us. Since their ship was equipped with the Drive, they were the only scouts I *had* to send across the Teegarden Expanse into Novan-claimed space to assess what we're up against and where the Armada was heading. It was all kept strictly secret—I'd wager there's only two or three people between Ranger central command and the Alliance's joint admiralty who knew they were working with me at all." The Admiral pauses for a moment, her tone growing more solemn. "Their last mission went... *badly*. The ship was captured, and later reported destroyed. We have no reason to believe there were any survivors."

Toreval hesitates for a moment, forcing themself to remain composed and centered. It isn't easy.

"...You didn't tell the Council this."

"They told me to wait and give my speech to the full Council, remember?"

"True."

The Admiral makes a vague gesture out towards the courtyard. "It's like you said, Youngest. Your people have been trying to integrate with our society. The Novans knew that most of our ships they'd encountered could outrun their striker raids and escape, and now it's certain they know *why*. Whether your Council agrees to help us openly or not, I doubt the Novans will care. I *still* don't believe that the 'Officially Non-Combatant Neutral/ Protected Species' status y'all have with the Greater Galactic Powers really means anything to them, frankly."

"I see." Toreval folds their upper pair of hands together contemplatively. Their tail swishes softly under the layers of their robes to match.

"You don't sound surprised."

"I'm not."

The Admiral looks back to them suspiciously. "If I didn't know better, Youngest, I'd say you already knew."

Toreval is silent for a few moments, all three of their eyes turned to watch the City. The bustle in the courtyard below them is comforting. Home has a rhythm of movement and sounds all its own; one that calms their thoughts in much the same way their meditations on the faraway sensation of the stars do. They often find themself seeking out high places from which to watch and soak it all in, especially when the weight of their responsibilities is particularly pressing. Over the last few months, Toreval has spent more time sitting on the roof of the Council House doing just that than they have in years.

"I did."

"*How*?" The Admiral is clearly taken aback. "Everything about it is top secret—"

"—Admiral." Toreval turns their third eye away from the city and looks straight into the alien's two green eyes, keeping their tone as level and pointed as they can. "Do you *really* think my kittens would not consult with me before volunteering for something so dangerous?"

The Admiral looks away, back towards the courtyard. "...I see."

Toreval falls silent once more, watching the human's bearing closely even as half of their mind is focused on keeping themself centered. They can't help but wonder what she's really feeling, considering how closely they understand she'd worked with Iralee and Inayan and the two young Rangers who'd become their counterparts scarcely three years before. Does it pain her, too, they wonder, to bear the weight of that loss?

"Was the information you gained worth their lives?" Toreval asks at last, calmly. Among the questions they've been waiting to ask the Admiral ever since the day the news reached them, this is the one that matters to them most. It's the one they can't help feeling that their kittens would have wanted them to ask.

"It's already saved us dozens of ships and their crews." The Admiral's voice remains even-toned, but with a touch of sadness. "We'd have lost countless more lives without them by now, I'm sure."

"I see."

"I'm sorry for your loss, Youngest. Teal and Turquoise were two of the best jumpers I've ever served with, even if I only knew them briefly."

Toreval gives the Admiral a little nod of acknowledgment. This is, they think, the first time they've heard their kittens' public names spoken aloud in months; the last was when the Ranger visited who brought them the two badges that now sit in their home beside a framed copy of the picture they'd taken the last time their whole family had been together. Losing Iralee and Inayan is still a fresh grief for them, but they appreciate her sentiment.

"They both always spoke highly of you, Admiral."

"I'm honored." The Admiral makes a similar slow nod in return. "They'd told me a few things about you as well, you know... I'd like to think we should have talked sooner than this."

"We should have," Toreval agrees, re-folding their upper pair of arms together over their chest, "but I doubt that would have changed anything."

"Probably not." The Admiral pauses, then tilts her head slightly to one side. "So you're aware of everything, then... Do you share their position about aiding us?"

Toreval considers their words carefully before answering. "What's best for my people may be very different from what I feel for myself."

The Admiral nods. "I can understand that."

"I'm sure you can."

"And surely you know what's at stake now—for all of us?"

"I do." Toreval's eyes stray back to the scene of the courtyard. "But what to do about it is something for the Council to decide."

"I suppose it is at that." The Admiral sighs lightly, shaking her head. "At any rate, I would welcome your support, Youngest."

"I'll let you know when I've *decided* to support you, Admiral."

Toreval slips down off the railing with another flutter of silks and across the vines to the courtyard below, leaving Admiral Marvin alone on the balcony.

Asimple change of clothes and jewelry later, and Toreval is ready for the next stage of their inquiry.

Their Elder's garb was hard-earned, but in this case it seems best to appear less formal. They want the person they'll be seeking out to be set at ease and inclined to be talkative when they introduce themself, and they're well aware that being immediately identifiable as the Council's Youngest might interfere with that. Knowing humans, too, they suspect that they'll appear as an entirely different person if dressed differently—after all, their own people are far more similar-looking on the whole than humans, aside from the shades of blue beneath their silver stripes.

Toreval can't deny that the idea of presenting themself as an ordinary young Florivan for an hour or two rather than the Elder they are *appeals* to them, although they don't have time at the moment to devote to pondering why that is.

In any case, it's off with the flowing layers of translucent amber silk, off with the matching beaded hood that covers everything behind the high tufted points of their ears, off with the veils and arm bands—and on with a simple yellow-embroidered grey tunic and matching loose-fitted trousers out of the box of things they'd kept from their younger days. They're surprised at first how well the clothes still fit, until they remember that their parent had insisted on sending them out to their apprenticeship with things they could 'grow into' without significant alteration. Toreval, though, never did have the chance to experience that final growth spurt that most kittens go through in their mid-adolescence; they only have to slightly unroll the cuffs of the trouser legs in the end.

Once it's all freed from their more ornate Elder's interlocking braids and bun and suitably brushed and tamed, Toreval pulls their waist-long silver hair back up into the same sort of triple-braid they once wore habitually. They fix everything in place behind their ears in a single simple loop with the old wooden hair pin and ring their parent had given them when they left for their apprenticeship. It's just as comfortable a hairstyle as they remember.

There's enough of a contrast in their appearance that when Toreval looks in the mirror after they've finished changing, *they* barely recognize that it's their own face looking back. In a way, they even feel a bit unlike themself. Was it really that long ago that they'd been the person who dressed like this and dreamed of traveling the stars?

Toreval sighs and turns away from the mirror to hang their Elder's garb up in their closet like they usually do before going to sleep. They know they can't let themself get caught up in thoughts today. They have too much work to do.

It's while they're folding the last of their veils that Toreval's keen catlike ears catch the sounds of their small home's garden door opening and familiar footsteps. In moments, the footsteps are coming up the stairs towards their family's nest room.

"Nida!" their surviving eldest kitten's voice calls as the footsteps approach, "I didn't expect you'd be home yet, but I saw your shoes by the door. Is—" The question hangs half-asked in the air. Their kitten stands in the nest room doorway, staring at Toreval with a particularly perplexed look on their softly greenish-blue face.

"'Is' what, Ilmi? Or who?" Toreval smiles at them and waves cheerfully with the tip of their tail, since all four of their hands are still busy folding the veil so it won't wrinkle.

"I... was going to ask if Taldee was up here with you..." Ilmi tilts their head to one side slightly, seeming to have lost their train of thought. They fold their lower pair of arms together over the soft amber of their tunic and make a vague gesture with one of their upper hands.

"No, I haven't seen them since the two of you came to meet me at the Council House for lunch." Toreval sets their neatly folded veil into its usual resting place on the side of the dressing table. Taldee is their youngest kitten, and despite their precocious curiosity is still young enough that they usually don't stray far from Ilmi. "I would have thought they were with you?"

"Well, they were *supposed* to be by now," says Ilmi, with a swish of their tail for punctuation. The bright-colored bangles they wear on their tail jingle from the motion. "I'd let them go to play with Elder Kyanite's kittens after we left you, since I needed to do some work for the festival preparations... but they were supposed to meet me for pre-lesson snacks half an hour ago and I still haven't seen them."

"They're probably still with the rest of the kittens, then." Toreval stifles a chuckle and comes over to set a reassuring hand on Ilmi's shoulder. Ilmi has always been far more conscious of time and appointments than their little sibling—or than either of their littermates, for that matter—but lately they've taken to worrying whenever Taldee is so much as a minute late to meet them. Toreval isn't worried, themself; they know that the rest of their extended family will be watching over Taldee just as they would any other Elder's kitten. Their city is safe, and their youngest is old enough to start to explore it with less supervision now. "I'm sure they'll turn up in time for your lessons."

"They'd better..." Ilmi lets out a soft sigh, then looks back to Toreval. "Especially since *you* seem to be up to something now too."

"Who, me?" Toreval reaches out with one of their upper hands to lightly ruffle Ilmi's ears. "Whatever gave you that idea?"

Ilmi leans into their touch contentedly, then looks up to them with the brow of their third eye pointedly raised. "Nida. *Really.* You're not wearing your robes and the suns are still out." Their lower two eyes trace up and down

Toreval's form. "You don't even have your hair the right way. What are you up to?"

Toreval smiles and makes a vague gesture at their outfit. "Oh, this? It's just a bit of Council business I'm seeing to, dear, that's all."

Ilmi continues giving them the look that says this explanation is *sorely* unsatisfactory. "What sort of Council business is it this time? You *never* go out dressed like this, even when you're planning mischief."

"A bit of information-gathering, that's all..." Toreval stifles a small laugh. "Stars, Ilmi, I promise it's nothing all that mischievous. I just need to be inconspicuous while I'm taking care of it, that's all."

Ilmi shakes their head with just a trace of amusement in the posture of their ears. "You're attempting to be subtle, today, then? Fine..." They go over to their own section of the closet and come back with an amber-dyed embroidered sash like the one they're wearing over their own tunic and hold it out to Toreval. "But at *least* you shouldn't go disowning yourself while you're being inconspicuous."

Toreval has to stifle another laugh while they're letting their eldest kitten tie the sash around their waist. "Thank you, Ilmi, I suppose you're right about that. Does this meet with your approval now?"

Ilmi looks them over again, then smirks and slips two bangles from the set they're wearing off their own tail and over the tuft of Toreval's. "Well, you look *different*... and I'm pretty sure anyone who didn't know us would mistake you for my older sibling... but at least you look like you're wearing a complete outfit now. So I suppose that's as good as I can ask for."

Toreval gives in to the impulse to hug their fully-grown kitten gladly. "Thank you, dear. Don't worry, I'll do my best not to cause too much trouble this afternoon."

Ilmi hugs them back, shaking their head lightly again. "You know you only ever say that before you *do* go and spread chaos, right?"

"Well... being the Council's pet troublemaker is part of my job, you know." Toreval ruffles Ilmi's hair again before releasing them from the hug. "At least until someone finally takes my place, that is."

"Nida," says Ilmi, showing the barest hint of a genuine smile, "I don't think it matters *who* winds up being Youngest after you. You'll always be the Council's troublemaker, one way or another."

"Maybe so." Toreval chuckles softly and heads towards the stairs with a jingling swish of their tail. "I'll send Taldee your way if I run into them."

"Thank you. Hopefully, they'll show up for their lessons *before* you have a chance to find them."

Toreval doesn't see it, but they know Ilmi probably has all four hands settled on their hips as they call this down the stairs. They smile to themself as they leave their house. Ilmi may be fully grown now, and a bit more fussy about things even than usual lately, but they're still the same sweetly contentious kitten they've always been—and Toreval couldn't be more proud.

IT DOESN'T TAKE TOREVAL LONG TO FIND WHERE the Admiral's young assistant has gone. There aren't more than a few hundred humans on the planet at any time, and even fewer in City-on-the-River itself. It's usually easy to ask after one in particular even based on a vague description.

In this case, it's *especially* easy, given that Toreval's own youngest has found the Ensign first.

Precocious kitten that they are, Taldee has even taken it upon themself to make contact and guide the somewhat lost human through the bustle of the city center. The two of them are easy to spot sitting on the wall of the fountain in the western square. It's an amusing image, really, with the little flurry of silver stripes and deep blue limbs barely contained in an amber-shaded tunic that is Taldee bouncing along the wall around the still figure of the

Ensign. The human's dark green and ivory uniform stands out from the crowd almost as much as his tawny-pale alien complexion and high-tied leaf-black hair do. He's taken the uniform jacket he was wearing in the Council Hall off now and has it loosely slung over one shoulder, exposing the crisp band-collared ivory shirt underneath.

From the look and sound of things as Toreval approaches the fountain, Taldee has been trying to educate the human on the proper way to eat their favorite frozen fruit off of its hanging string. They can't help being amused by that. Leave it to their youngest to find a way to get an extra afternoon snack out of a supposed tourist.

"There you are, Lapis!" Toreval calls as they approach, using their kitten's public name. "I was wondering where you'd gotten to."

Taldee hears them and immediately brightens, waving excitedly with all four hands and their tail. "Look, Nida! I found this lost human!"

"So I see, kitten." Toreval chuckles, coming to stand beside where their youngest is still perched on the wall. "You have a new friend, then?"

"He was wanting to see more of the city, so I'm showing him!"

"I see. Good for you, Lapis, I'm glad you could help him." Toreval lays one of their lower hands atop their kitten's head and ruffles the short locks of silver hair behind Taldee's perked-up ears. That's another point of oddity with the humans, of course; human ears are so strangely shaped and low on the sides of their faces and can't move at all, much less independently to focus on specific sounds like the softly pointed pinnae their people have.

Taldee's long tufted tail waves happily in response. They have no idea yet just how helpful their befriending the young human has been, of course, but they seem pleased enough with the praise all the same.

"Now," says Toreval, shifting their tone to something ever-so-slightly more firm, "I *believe* you have lessons this afternoon? Jade mentioned when I saw them that you were supposed to have met up with them already."

"Um... right! Lessons! I almost forgot!" Taldee scampers down from the fountain wall and turns to the human, holding all four of their hands clasped behind their back. "Sorry, Hsu Li, I guess I can't show you the whole city today after all..."

"Don't worry, Lapis," Toreval assures them, "I'm sure you'll see your new friend again later—and I'll take care of showing him around. Now run along before you're actually late and Jade comes looking for you. You *know* how they feel about tardiness."

Taldee wastes no time in exchanging a hurried goodbye with the Ensign and scurrying off, their tail still swishing excitedly behind them. Toreval is already looking forward to hearing what their youngest has to say about the human tonight. Taldee is quite observant, after all, when they want to be.

The Ensign looks to Toreval now, raising an eyebrow. "The schools here don't run through the full day, then?"

"Kittens of Lapis' age take lessons in the afternoon and evenings with their littermates under a mentor their parent has chosen. We give them the rest of the day to play and pursue their own interests." Toreval smiles lightly and tilts their head to one side. "A bit different than what your people do, I understand?"

"Very. Our system's a bit more… standardized. Efficient universal education and all that."

"So I've heard." Toreval remembers quite a few stories from their days as an apprentice about what schooling is like for most humans. *Rigid* and *overly categorical* are the words they used to associate with it, more than not.

"Well, it works well enough for us." The Ensign gives them a bit of a good-natured shrug. "And I suppose your way must work for you too."

"It does."

The Ensign glances back towards where Taldee has disappeared into the crowd, then chuckles lightly. "I will say, I almost pity the teacher who has to keep a whole family like that one focused long enough to educate them. Regular little lightning ball, that kid, and I mean that in the nicest way."

Toreval has never heard a more appropriate analogy for their youngest. Taldee has been more of a handful even from the day their eyes opened than their three older siblings had been combined. That in itself is somewhat remarkable, too, considering that Ilmi is the only one of their kittens who has never seemed to have inherited the penchant for 'overly adventuresome trouble-making' that Toreval themself is so often teased for having.

"I definitely know what you mean," Toreval says, holding back a laugh. "Lapis is currently studying under their older sibling, actually, and they don't have any littermates… but fortunately for Jade's sanity, Lapis will be old enough to be apprenticed for their training in the Strange in a year or two."

There's a strong imprint between Toreval's two surviving offspring, but they know Ilmi will be relieved when the day comes for someone else to be charged with Taldee's education. It's good practice for Ilmi, though, since they're being trained as one of the star-keeping storytellers who preserve their people's history and traditions. If Ilmi can handle their 'lightening ball' of a younger sibling, they'll be well prepared for teaching any litter of kittens they're tasked with mentoring in the future.

"You start them working in Quantum Space that *young?*" The Ensign's eyes widen slightly.

"Of course." Toreval can't help being amused by his use of the more scientific-sounding name the humans have given the veiled dimension that's so much a part of the Florivan way of life. "Apprentices stay with their spacefaring mentors for several years—once they're finished with that, they'll be ready to find counterparts for themselves and go on to become part of a starship's crew or take a position here in the Sanctuary or at one of your people's academic institutions to train for further development of other skills like Jade has. Some do both." They pause, making a vague gesture at the bustle of people passing through the courtyard around them. "Not all of us will choose Navigators and go wandering, in the end, but the skills for dipping into the Strange safely are something we all have to learn."

"I see." The Ensign dips his head briefly. "Forgive me, I'm not as familiar with your people's ways as I'd like to be."

Toreval looks the human over closely. They don't think they will ever fully become accustomed to the lack of a third eye with this species, as it makes it so difficult to know where to focus their own gaze at times—and yet, the aesthetic effect of the Ensign's deep brown irises is striking. An alien face, for sure, but not an unpleasant one.

"So, Hsu Li, is it?" Toreval smiles and brightens their tone to show him they weren't offended by the questions. "I believe I now owe you a tour of the city on Lapis' behalf."

"Just Li is fine. 'Hsu' is my family name." The Ensign smiles lightly himself, and then hesitates. "And I'd be glad to take that tour, if it's not an inconvenience to you. I'm sure I can find my way around, otherwise…"

"I assure you, it will be my pleasure."

"Then thank you." The Ensign absently shakes out his jacket and re-folds it back over his other shoulder. "I have to admit, it's my first time visiting Procyon—and I didn't expect to have free time enough to see the sights."

Toreval makes a pleased swishing gesture with their tail. "Well, then, I'm glad to have the chance to show them to you."

"Thank you." The Ensign offers a hand to them. "And what do I call you?"

"Celadon is fine."

Toreval accepts the brief handshake. His hand is strange, with the extra finger, and looks even more alien against their own four pale blue-green digits—alien, and unexpectedly but pleasantly warm.

"Nice to meet you, Celadon."

"Likewise, Li."

Toreval gestures for him to follow as they walk down a side street. They smile softly to themself now.

Somehow, Toreval is already looking forward to getting to know this young human better.

THE LOW GARDENS BY THE RIVERSIDE HAVE ALWAYS been among Toreval's favorite places in City-on-the-River. There's always something sweet-smelling blooming on the archways of the various terraces leading down to the wide stone paths which run along the riverbank as it winds through the middle of the city. Among the terraces, too, there are many lovely shaded courtyards amidst the plants where one can sit and watch the people passing by and the bright-colored drama of the slim-winged water skimmer lizards diving to catch fish from the current.

This evening, just as the suns are beginning to set, Toreval is sitting with the Ensign on one of the swing benches in one of the lower courtyards on the Council House side of the river. They've had more of a good time than they expected they would walking around the city with the young human and pointing out the major landmarks like the Star-Keepers' library and the different bridges and plazas which mark the six neighborhoods around the city's center and the Council House.

"Well, Li?" Toreval looks to their new acquaintance over the rim of a cup of spiced tea they'd acquired at a nearby refreshment center on their way to the riverside courtyard. "Do you think you can keep yourself oriented now for the rest of your time here?"

The Ensign softly blows the steam off of his own tea before answering. "I think so—this part of your city, at least. I'd probably get a bit lost again if I strayed much further from what you've shown me."

Toreval nods, mentally noting that much of their day's work as a success. They haven't gotten much *information* out of the Ensign yet, but at least now they've made contact with him and clearly presented themself as a person open to being befriended and showing him around. They're sure that will encourage him to be more open with them in the future, particularly considering that the Admiral has all but given him orders to 'get to know the locals.'

"Hmm... I can show you more while you're here, if you like. The Sanctuary's largest arboretum isn't far from the borders of where we've already walked, and I'm sure you'll like that." Toreval sets down their tea on the little table to the side of the swing bench and pulls up a map of their home on the projected holoscreen of their little spherical pocket-com. "See? This is where we are now," they say, gesturing at the appropriate place on the map, "and the City Arboretum is here near the cliffs upriver on the far bank—the area of forest there behind its main buildings is a nature preserve, too. If you like hiking at all, the trails there are nice."

"I do, actually." The Ensign pauses to take a sip from his tea, then looks back to Toreval. "I wouldn't want to impose on you, though—I'm sure you have more important things to do than play 'tour guide' for me."

Toreval chuckles. Technically, they probably do have other matters that they might attend to instead; the Youngest's tasks aren't only ceremonial, after all, but none of those are particularly pressing at the moment. "Oh, it's not an imposition at all. I'd be delighted to take you. Hospitality is a virtue we value, you know."

"I can see that it is." The Ensign looks back down to their map. "Do you get many lost 'tourists' around here, then?"

"A few here and there. Usually, humans who come to our Sanctuary are part of the crews of visiting starships— they're brought down as guests of the Elder whose household the ship's jumper belongs to, though, so they'll be shown around by members of that family. Such guests are seldom left to get lost."

"That's quite a high honor, Celadon, isn't it? Even for people the jumper doesn't work directly with?"

"We take our friendship with your people quite seriously." Toreval makes a small shrug and picks their teacup back up with their tail so they can take a sip. "It's something of a rare treat for me to get to be the one 'playing tour guide,' as you put it."

"Oh?" The Ensign takes on a hint of a smirk now over the rim of his own cup. "You're good at it—I would have thought you were more experienced."

Toreval finds themself amused by the notion; it's been *years* since they've been asked by anyone to escort a visitor around the city casually like this. Being the Council's official liaison to the Sol Coalition diplomats who visit on occasion and making sure they get from place to place doesn't quite count, in their mind. Toreval's duties in that regard are usually to coordinate the *other* people who are serving as the visitors' direct guides.

"My family—the household I belong to—is... well, rather small, now." Toreval catches themself mid-sentence just before they slip and potentially give their identity away. "All of us live here in City-on-the-River. No jumpers in the mix to bring down tourists for us these days, I'm afraid." Toreval holds back a sigh and does their best not to let themself be swept up by the memories of the last visitors their household *did* have, and how happy they'd all been showing Iralee and Inayan's Ranger counterparts their home. They stare out at the dances of the skimmer-lizards on the water for a moment before they speak again. "I... usually only get called on when there's someone who *wouldn't* otherwise be the guest of a particular Elder's household who requires a guide. That doesn't happen often."

When their third eye glances in the Ensign's direction, he meets it with a sympathetic softness in his own dark brown pair. Toreval isn't sure why.

"That's what, then..." the Ensign begins, casually and without any hint to suggest he has intention to probe them further on the matter of their family, "people who come here as passengers rather than crew members?"

"Essentially, yes."

"Well, I'd say it's appropriate you're the one who Lapis passed me off to after they found me wandering around lost earlier, isn't it?" The Ensign flashes Toreval a conspiratorial smile. "Since *I'm* one of those unclaimed visitors who occasionally become your responsibility and all."

"I suppose it is at that." Toreval finds themself matching his expression. It's quite pleasing that his conclusions align so neatly with their own plan to gain his confidence.

"I'm surprised we weren't assigned someone already, of course." Li glances out towards the water just as one of the brilliantly red skimmer-lizards makes a dive into the current after a fish with a magnificent splash. "Or the Admiral hasn't told me yet if we have been, at any rate."

"I'm sure the Elders have made arrangements for her as a diplomatic guest," Toreval replies. "Even if the two of you are here on leave."

Thinking back, Toreval is reasonably sure that Admiral Marvin has yet to inform the Council whether or not she'll require a guide while she's a guest of the Sanctuary. Her visit had come so secretly and on relatively short notice compared to other honored diplomatic guests that even the arrangements for her accommodations while she's visiting were only being made this afternoon. She and her assistant, though, *are* here as guests of the Council itself rather than any specific Elder's household. Toreval makes a mental note to see what they can do about double-checking what arrangements have been made for the two of them in the morning.

"Ah, probably." The Ensign nods. "Well, if it's not an imposition, then, I'd be happy to accept."

"Wonderful." Toreval's ears twitch softly to match their pleased expression. They gesture to the map on their holoscreen again. "I can meet you there tomorrow, if you think you can find your way by yourself. Or would you rather I collect you from the bridge here?"

The Ensign considers the map for a few moments. "Depending on where I'm supposed to be staying, I should be able to find my way now that I've had a look at a proper map..." He lets out a small self-deprecating chuckle. "But the bridge sounds like a better plan. I *know* I can find that for sure."

"All right, then. Shall we say mid-morning? I should be done with the few things I have to attend to by then." Toreval deactivates their holoscreen and slips the little spherical device back into one of their tunic's pockets.

"That works for me. As far as I know, unless the Admiral comes up with any paperwork she needs me to sort for her, I have nothing to do but wait until your Council is finally ready to properly hear her." The Ensign takes another small sip from his tea.

Toreval does likewise, then looks to him with a curious tilt of their head. "That's your role, then? Handling paperwork?"

"To a certain extent. My official title is 'Personal Assistant to the Admiral,'" the Ensign says with a smirk and small air quotation gestures for emphasis, "but in practice it's a mix of glorified map-reading, paperwork... and making sure there's always coffee ready for her right before she thinks to ask for it."

"I get the impression you do a good job at that." Toreval can't resist smirking back at him.

"That's what I've been doing ever since I graduated from the Fleet Academy three years ago." The Ensign shrugs lightly. "I'm still not sure why Admiral Marvin picked me, but I couldn't ask for a better officer to serve under."

Toreval's third eye traces over the Ensign's face. They knew that their new human acquaintance was *young*, but they didn't realize until just now quite *how* young he really is. "Why do I have the impression you graduated *early*?"

The Ensign gives them that same cheerful smirk again. "Technically? I ended up signing to the Fleet for the two-year reserve technical officer program after my letters disqualified me for the track I'd applied to in the Civilian Space Service Academy, and it's not exactly my fault that I turned eighteen the week *after* graduation... or that the Admiral issued my assignment orders the day of." He pauses for a moment, then shrugs. "That was before the War, though. The Fleet's changed their age restrictions since then."

Toreval shakes their head, stifling a chuckle. If they've done the math right, this means the Ensign is all of twenty now at the most; roughly three years older than their eldest kittens. It's no wonder Taldee was drawn to him—and no wonder Toreval themself is intrigued. If anyone among their people knows what it's like to be *young* for the position of high responsibility they've found themself in, it's Toreval.

"No, I don't suppose that your birthday was something you could control. But you're content with your position?"

"I am." The Ensign looks back out over the water, where the skimmer-lizards are now retreating to the branches of the nearby blossom-covered trees for the evening. "I never thought I'd be standing by the Admiral's side during anything but peacetime, though. There's a lot more to the job than I ever expected, thanks to the Novans."

Toreval follows his gaze, nodding slowly. "I think I understand what you mean."

The Ensign seems about to say something more, but a chime from a small device in his own pocket distracts him. After checking the message it's alerted him to, he taps out a response on the small green-toned holoscreen and slips it back into place. This done, he looks up to Toreval. "I don't suppose you know where the 'Courtyard of the Ruby-fruit Tree' by the Council House is?"

"I do." Toreval chuckles. They spent quite a lot of time as a kitten *climbing* the tree in question. "That's where you and your Admiral have been placed, then?"

"Yeah—from what she's said, there's a guesthouse there?"

"There is." Toreval stands, pausing to drink the last of their tea. "It's mainly used for honored guests of the Council. Would you like me to escort you there?"

"If you don't mind." The Ensign stretches as he, too, stands from the swing-bench. "I think I remember it from your map, but having someone to show me the way is better."

Toreval offers the young human one of their lower arms. "I'd be delighted. I don't live very far from there myself, actually."

"Well, now, that's a convenient coincidence." The Ensign takes their arm and follows them up the stairs from the courtyard towards the higher terraces.

Toreval shoots him a conspiratorial smirk of their own. "Haven't you ever heard that Florivans don't tend to believe in coincidences?"

"Once, but not from one of you directly. What is it, if not a coincidence, then?"

"Oh... something pleasantly unlikely that's still meant to be, I suppose, is the simple way of putting it."

"That's not the same thing?"

"If you want it to be, Li." Toreval shrugs, stifling a giggle. "We're too used to the Strange arranging things for us to really expect the Normal to act any differently, even if it's all beyond our understanding in the moment."

The Ensign raises his eyebrows curiously. "You say that as if Quantum Space has a will and agency in itself?"

"It likes us to think that it does." The bangles Ilmi had placed on Toreval's tail earlier jingle brightly as it swishes behind them with a carefree teasing motion. "I'd offer to introduce you, but you *are* human, after all."

The Ensign shakes his head in an amused way that makes his long high-tied ponytail swish almost in time with the motion of Toreval's tail. "I'm afraid I'll have to decline that offer if you ever make it—the Admiral *does* prefer me with my brain intact, you know—and I've heard too many stories about what happens to folks who get too close to even small miasma leaks."

"As you wish, then." Toreval takes on their most formally reassuring tone. "We don't tend to have miasma clouds around the Sanctuary, but I'll be sure to steer you around them at a safe distance if I notice one."

"Thanks, Celadon." The Ensign's eyes are sparkling now with a mirthful glint, even though he seems to be trying to sound formal as well. "I appreciate that."

"Now, some friends of mine run a *lovely* little bakery not far from your accommodations that doesn't close until well after sunset..." Toreval smiles up at him. "If you don't mind, I'd like to take a small detour to pick up some pastries to take back to the rest of my household."

"Sounds good to me. If they have anything more savory, I might get one or two to take back to the Admiral myself." The Ensign chuckles. "That might make up for the fact that I can't exactly bring her coffee around here."

"Oh, you'll like this place, then! The friends of mine who run it are a retired jumper and their counterpart—the two of them have a special permit from the Council to import and serve coffee to visiting humans." Toreval twitches their ears lightly. It's a long-standing point of curious amusement for them that one of the handful of Earth-origin plants that's so *incredibly* poisonous for their species—even if it is good-smelling—is the preferred beverage of the majority of Navigators and many other humans. They're not surprised, somehow, that the Admiral is among those who seem to be fueled by the stuff.

"Really?" Judging by the clear elation in the Ensign's voice, he has more than a small fondness for coffee himself. "I'll be *very* pleased to be introduced to your friends, then."

Toreval's tail makes another jingling amused swish. "I had a feeling you would be."

A SMALL SET OF BELLS RING ON THE DOOR AS Toreval and the Ensign enter the bakery. The smell of fresh breads and confections wafts around them like a comforting, yeasty embrace. Toreval's been coming here since they were a kitten. The vibrant tapestry-draped walls and soft piles of cushions under the windows feel just as much like home as their little house does.

"Well, Li," they say, making a grand gesture at the small but neatly-arranged space, "here we are! What do you think?"

"It smells wonderful, for one thing." The Ensign surveys the room appreciatively.

"Indi!" The tall, pale human woman behind the counter swings her brightly blond braid over her shoulder and calls towards the beaded curtain separating the bakery's sitting area from the workroom. "Donnie's here—they brought a *friend*!"

"Now, Monica," Toreval laughs, coming over to lean on the counter on their lower set of elbows. "Is this *really* so unusual?"

Monica arches an eyebrow at them pointedly as her sparkling blue eyes look them up and down, then glance to the Ensign. She's a human of few words, usually, but that doesn't stop her from being able to get a point across when she wants to. In this case, Toreval can clearly interpret the look: "You are dressed differently and have a new human with you, silly kitten, what do *you* think?"

Toreval just smiles and shakes their head in response. The woman has always been as dear to them as any of their entiles or older siblings—and just as much a mentor as her counterpart was when they were Taldee's age. They're only grateful that she's never taken to using their title, since that habit now is preventing her from accidentally giving them away to the Ensign.

"You know, Monica," they hear Indigo Taivin's voice say over the jingling of the curtain of beads, "one of these days, they're going to finally grow into the formalities and—" Indigo halts mid-sentence as they enter the room, all three eyes slightly widened when they meet Toreval's. "Ah." The older Florivan's eyes settle into a more curiously amused than disapproving expression. "Well, then. Good evening, *Donnie*. You're here for Ril-nut buns?"

Toreval holds back a sigh of relief that Indigo also isn't making a fuss about their disguise in front of the Ensign. "Yes, if you still have any—and I *may* have told

Li here about the wonders of your potato-and-ulinroot pasties."

Indigo shakes their head with a decidedly amused swish of their tail, then dusts their upper hands off on the apron they're wearing over their brilliantly red tunic. "If I know you, you really lured him here on the promise of coffee."

The Ensign chuckles softly. "Celadon *did* mention you were one of the only people on the planet who served it, yes, but I have to say the description of the baked goods was equally tempting..."

Indigo looks him over for a moment, then smiles and approaches to offer him a lightly flour-dusted hand. "I think I'm going to like you, Ensign...?"

"Hsu Li," he replies, accepting the handshake. "But I'm off-duty at the moment, so just Li is fine."

"Nice to meet you, Li. You can call me Indigo, and this..." Indigo nods their head in the direction of their counterpart. "...Is my Navigator, Monica Malarius. She can sort out whatever your preferred poison is for you."

Monica gives a little wave of acknowledgment in his direction.

The Ensign waves back with a charming smile. "I'd appreciate that. I'm sure the Admiral will too, if you don't mind me taking her some. It's a bit late in the evening, of course, but we're both still running on ship's time at the moment."

"By all means. You're Admiral Marvin's, then?" Indigo tilts their head to one side curiously. Their third eye gives Toreval an equally curious and pointed look.

"Her assistant." The Ensign doesn't seem to notice the shift in Indigo's expression. "Celadon has been kind enough to show me the lay of the land while I had a bit of free time."

"I see." Indigo smiles and finally releases the Ensign's hand. "You and your Admiral are both welcome here as long as we happen to be open. Now, why don't you let Monica show off her coffee setup for you—she roasts the beans herself, even—while I sort Donnie out with those pastries in the back?"

"Thank you." The Ensign gives a little bow of gratitude in Indigo's direction and then follows Monica down to the other end of the counter.

"Donnie?" Indigo parts the beaded curtain and gestures pointedly with their tail for Toreval to follow.

Toreval forces the sigh they're holding in to turn into a chuckle instead. They know that tone of voice *far* too well. "Right behind you."

Indigo leads Toreval into the back of the bakery to the chairs and table at the far end beside the old stone oven which one of their mutual ancestors had built at the founding of City-on-the-River and gestures for them to take a seat. They pause to make sure the loaves of crusty seed-bread sitting in the oven aren't burning, then look back to Toreval with their lower pair of hands on their hips.

"So. What are you up to, Toreval?" Indigo narrows all three of their eyes, just like they used to do whenever they found a certain trio of naughty kittens playing in their flour bins. They cross their upper pair of arms over their chest, although their tail is still swishing with a silent amusement.

Toreval can't help giggling.

It's nice that there's at least one person in their life who still calls them by their private name sometimes, even if Indigo tends only to use it when they're baffled like this. "You know, Ilmi asked me the same thing when I left the house?"

"I'm not surprised. That kitten of yours has more sense than *you* ever have—I'm amazed they let you leave at all, dressed like that." Indigo raises an eyebrow.

"They helped me fix the outfit, actually—but I promise, I'm not really 'up to' anything..." Toreval hesitates lightly. "I just needed to be less conspicuous for the afternoon, that's all."

Indigo shakes their head, although their ears twitch with obvious amusement now in front of the red bandanna that's keeping their hair neatly out of the way. "You haven't decided *what* you're up to yet, then. Got it. And the human kid you brought in... he doesn't know who you are?"

"No, I haven't told him." Toreval absently runs the tuft of their tail through the fingers of their lower pair of hands. "And I'd prefer he didn't know—not yet, at any rate."

Indigo comes over and sets a hand on their shoulder gently, their eyes softening. "Aliren told me about the Admiral's visit earlier when they came by to pick up their kittens after the Council session. If this is some of your Elder's business connected to all of that, don't worry, we won't interfere."

Toreval looks up to their old mentor with a slight nod. Aliren—Elder Woad, properly—is Indigo's youngest sibling. Indigo had retired from active service as a starship's QSD engineer and returned to the Sanctuary to join Elder Woad's newly-formed household. Monica, ever the loyal counterpart, had come with them. Toreval was just a small kitten, then. They do consider Elder Woad a friend as well, now, although the two of them have never been particularly close.

"Thank you," Toreval says, softly. "I'll admit it's partially personal business as well, but please believe me when I say that what I'm doing is *important*."

"I don't doubt that it is." Indigo smiles and gives their shoulder a light, reassuring squeeze, then goes over to a nearby set of cooling racks to fill a small basket with Toreval's favorite freshly-baked pastries. "Your young Ensign seems nice—do you know if he's been trained for Nav? He has the voice for it."

"Li isn't *mine*, but he's turned out to be pleasant company." Toreval stifles a chuckle. "He didn't mention if he had—I suppose you'd have to ask him—but I have to agree, he does have a rather bright voice, doesn't he?"

"I just might do that. Who knows, maybe *he'll* be the one who finally gets little Ilmi out into the stars for you." Indigo shoots them a teasing smirk as they present the filled and neatly cloth-wrapped basket. "Well, at any rate, this is the happiest I've seen you in *months*. It's good to have you causing mischief again—even if I don't know what that is this time."

Toreval rolls their third eye, but then finds themself staring down at the basket in their hands and letting out an unexpected sigh. They weren't expecting such a flood of conflicting emotions to run through them all at once. They can't even identify half of what they're feeling.

"Toreval?" Indigo's hands lightly settle on theirs, pulling them back into reality with an unmistakably concerned expression on their face.

"I'm fine." Toreval dabs a bit of unexpected moisture out of the corners of their eyes. "It's just been a long day, that's all."

Just as they once did whenever Toreval as a kitten was overwhelmed by one of their lessons for reasons that had little to do with the lesson itself, Indigo folds them up into a hug before they even realize how badly they need one. Their old mentor still smells the same, too, like flour and spices and traces of Monica's ever-present coffee aromas.

Toreval clings to them for a moment, then finds it in themself to smile and dust off the flour that's now covering their own clothes once they've let go.

"Don't mind me, I'm just letting myself dwell on things too much again... although I have to admit, it's been kind of nice this afternoon not having to be *me* for a little while."

"Now really," says Indigo, giggling softly as they brush a bit of flour off of Toreval's cheek, "*you* might see a difference right now, but robes or not, you're still the cheeky kitten who I used to have to chase all over the city just so they'd wear themself out enough that I could get them to sit still for their lessons. You're the same mischievous little scamp even when you're sitting up there in the Council House with Aliren and the others, even if you do a good job of hiding it."

Toreval catches the giggle themself. "Thanks, Indigo. I... needed to hear that, I think."

"I'm not surprised you did. Now..." Indigo picks up another small basket, "help me pick out some pastries for your new friend to take back to his Admiral, will you? I have plenty to choose from—and if you happen to want to *sample...*"

"Of course!" Toreval follows with a cheerful swish of their tail. "We can't go sending the Council's guests pastries that haven't been checked, after all."

Indigo flashes a conspiratorial grin. "I had a feeling you'd say that."

When Toreval returns to their home, both of their kittens are sitting at the high wooden table in the family kitchen. Ilmi looks to be reading over something on their pocket-com's holoscreen, while Taldee is hard at work finishing some assignment or other on their little datapad. Both of them look up at the sound of the door.

Taldee immediately abandons their datapad and scampers over to wrap all four arms around Toreval's legs. The kitten's tail is waving excitedly to match the expression of their face.

"Nida! You're home! Did you have fun?" Before Toreval can answer, Taldee's already moved on to more questions. "Ooh! That's one of Entile Indigo's baskets, isn't it? Did you say hi to them and Auntie Monica for me? What's in the basket?" Taldee curiously lifts the edge of the covering cloth. "Is it for *us*? Are they making buns for the River Festival yet?"

Toreval can't help giggling as they affectionately ruffle their youngest's ears.

"Settle down, kitten—yes, Indigo sent you and Ilmi some Ril-nut buns..." They look over to meet their older kitten's amused smirk with a teasing grin of their own. "...*And* some of those spiced buns Monica makes, too."

Ilmi seems to be trying to conceal how excited they are when Toreval sets the basket down in front of them, but the jingling swish of their tail is a clear giveaway. Monica's ancient family recipes have been irresistible to them ever since they first opened their eyes. As a kitten, they were never quite as much of a handful as their two littermates *except* when presented with an opportunity to sample her baking—Toreval has more than one picture of Ilmi as a small fuzzy silver thing peering up from the depths of a basket full of the retired Navigator's cardamom and cinnamon buns after they'd slipped in and refused to emerge until there were only crumbs left in there with them.

"You brought me kanelbullar so I'll leave the questions to Taldee?" Ilmi raises all three eyebrows in a manner that's more amused than accusatory. They're already neatly lifting the cloth off of the basket and folding it.

"Well..." Toreval smiles and gives Ilmi's ears a light affectionate ruffling, just as they had Taldee's. "Think of it as a gesture of thanks for letting me borrow your sash."

Ilmi unconsciously leans into Toreval's touch for a moment. They may be fully grown now, but they're still a sweet, affectionate little kitten at heart. "We can call it that for *now...* but I still want to know what you've been up to all afternoon."

Taldee, meanwhile, hops back up onto their stool at the table and reaches over to slip one of the fluffy golden Ril-nut buns out of the basket. They happily begin nibbling at the crisp outer edges of the nut-paste-filled pastry.

Toreval chuckles and takes one of the same buns for themself. They take a seat on the stool beside Ilmi and lean over to look at Taldee's upside-down datapad. "So, what are you two working on this evening?"

Ilmi shoots them a silent look that says that their attempt to change the subject is *noticed*, but the neatly swirled golden sweet roll decorated with pearl sugar that they're now holding between their upper pair of hands has, in fact, placated them for the moment. Toreval has the distinct impression that they'll be facing all of the questions their older kitten is holding back before long, though. Ilmi seldom forgets things like that.

"Ilmi's making me help with *their* assignments," says Taldee with an adorably annoyed twitch of their ears.

Ilmi rolls their lower two eyes in response, the third one still focused on the kanelbulle in their hands. "Asking you to write a few paragraphs about your favorite story from our people's history is *hardly* making you do my homework, Taldee. It just happens to be that you're studying the same stuff Star-Keepers like me train in, that's all—and *you're* the one who decided to write about a story I'm performing at the River Festival."

"But you didn't let me pick my *real* favorite!" Taldee pouts, looking over to Toreval with a wide, pleading look that they know all too well. "I like the story you're going to recite at the Festival, but it's *not* my favorite."

"There's dozens of other tales in the River Cycle you could have chosen—"

"—But *they're* not my favorite either!"

Toreval looks between their kittens, then shakes their head in amusement and gets up again to make a pot of tea for their family to share along with the pastries. "Which story *is* your favorite, then, Taldee? I know Ilmi wouldn't outright forbid you to study anything without talking to me first..."

"It's the one about the last Beacon!" Taldee replies excitedly, "and how Midnight Amaril made friends with her and now we *all* get to have human friends if we want to and take them for our counterparts!"

A glance in Taldee's direction shows that the kitten's tail is swishing with gleeful interest and their ears are perked up—and that Ilmi is now lightly rubbing at their temples with their free hand.

"I didn't say you *couldn't* write about something from the Beacon Cycle or the first contact we had with modern humans, Taldee—just that you need to learn about the other stories *too* and this is a good time to do that because the River Festival is coming up and you'll be able to see all of the Cycle performances then."

"You *said* I had to write about a story that didn't have humans in it." Taldee is still making their adorable pouting face. "I like the human stories better—they're not dusty and old."

"Taldee..." Ilmi's tone says they've likely already had this conversation with their younger sibling several times today. Toreval's always amazed by the amount of restraint Ilmi has when dealing with things like this, especially considering how young they are, but it's clear they're starting to lose patience.

"Now, kittens," says Toreval, still more amused than anything by the whole exchange. They bring the teapot and cups over, pouring some for their kittens and setting the smooth stoneware cups of steaming amber liquid down beside each of them with a light clink. They sit back down on the stool beside Ilmi and pour a cup for themself. "No need to argue about this. Taldee, sweetheart, part of your education *is* to learn our people's old stories and traditions so you can pass them on to others someday. That's just as important a part of things as all of the scientific and mathematical studies you do—and all of your lessons to do with working in the Strange. Ilmi's only trying to make sure you don't neglect the subjects that aren't your favorites."

Taldee sighs, then nods and dunks a bit of pinched-off Ril-nut bun into their tea before nibbling at it. "Yes, Nida..."

"And Ilmi," Toreval continues, turning and setting a hand on one of their older kitten's free ones, "as long as your sibling *does* finish the assignment you've given them, I don't see any harm in letting them write a *second* one about whichever story they like too—and having them go talk to Indigo and Monica about their firsthand experience training under Midnight and Miss Lin as well, as part of that report. Our friendship with the humans is undeniably a big part of our world too, and exploring our history with them can only serve to prepare Taldee for working with them in the future."

Ilmi also sighs, swishing their tail with a lightly jingling agitation. "Yes, Nida."

"Now, can you both be satisfied with that?"

Both kittens nod, then busy themselves with nibbling on their pastries and pointedly not saying anything. Toreval considers this as good a response as they could have hoped for. Taldee's curiosity about the world and the aliens their people have begun to integrate their society with is inexhaustible, after all—and so is Ilmi's discomfort at the notion of having another of their siblings so obviously set on making the Navigator's compact with a human someday and leaving Procyon for the stars. It's inevitable that the two of them have little disagreements like this, anymore.

Toreval nibbles at their own Ril-nut bun, savoring the lightly sweet flavor and smooth texture of the filling. After taking a sip from their tea, they turn their eyes over to the shimmering holoscreen in front of Ilmi with a smile. "So, Ilmi, you're working on Festival preparations?"

Ilmi nods again, pausing to peel another of the swirled layers off of their own pastry. "I am. Elder Kyanite sent me their notes on the role I'm responsible for during the opening performance. They didn't have many changes to suggest to my draft of the choreography, but there *were* enough that I'm having to correct that I'll need to re-memorize it... and then I need to spend the next couple of days working on the star-keeping sphere the Eldest has asked me to make for the closing performance as well."

"Sounds like you'll be busy, then." Toreval gives Ilmi's shoulder a reassuring pat. "But also that you've got everything well in hand."

"I hope so." Ilmi looks up to them with just the barest hint of a wry smirk. "Especially because you'll look awfully silly standing up there on the stage with the Eldest at the closing if I *don't* get a proper sphere made to present to the two of you."

Toreval stifles a giggle. "And then everyone will start up teasing me again about that time when Laryven and Liret and I were kittens and we scampered off with one of the ones that was supposed to be used that year and hid it in our little nest of shiny things in the rafters of the Eldest's office and no one knew what had happened with it for *months...*"

"How *did* they find it, then?" asks Taldee, their usual curiosity sparkling in their eyes once again.

Ilmi shakes their head, although Toreval is sure they're doing their best not to laugh. "From what Elder Kyanite's told me, it rolled *out* of the rafters and landed in the Eldest's teacup in the middle of a meeting—and then Nida here scampered over and promptly tried to retrieve it and hide it again... and got themself *soaked* in tea in the process."

"In my defense," says Toreval, letting out a self-deprecating chuckle, "I hadn't even lost my first patches of fur yet—and I couldn't actually lift the thing without Laryven and Liret helping me, much less climb all the way up into the rafters while carrying it." They pause to take a sip from their tea and give Ilmi a light, playful nudge with the fluff on the tip of their tail. "Unlike *one* little kitten I knew who would disappear every time I had to go into the

Star-Keepers' Archives and convince their littermates to help them roll every sphere they could find into the nearest corner so they could use them for a nest..."

Ilmi nudges them back, flashing just a hint of a smile. "I don't know *who* you could possibly be talking about, Nida. All of your kittens are every bit as well-behaved as you are."

Toreval can't help giggling at that. "Of *course* you are, dear..." They reach over and ruffle Ilmi's ears again, just for good measure. "Now, since you have such a busy week ahead of you, would it help if I keep Taldee with me tomorrow so you can focus on all of that?"

"Don't you have Council business going on?" Ilmi twitches an ear at them.

"Well, yes, but it's nothing that having them along would interfere with." Toreval smiles and looks over to their youngest kitten. "What do you say, Taldee? Do you think you could stand doing some observational lessons with me instead tomorrow?"

Taldee perks up, their tail swishing excitedly. "Can I?"

"As long as you finish writing that assignment *tonight*," says Ilmi, tapping the table in front of Taldee's datapad. "And then you can take notes on whatever Nida shows you tomorrow and tell me about what you learned." They tilt their head lightly to one side as they speak with the serious 'kitten mentor' tone they've been developing ever since Toreval first asked them to take charge of their little sibling's education. "Deal?"

"Deal!" Taldee bounces up from their stool and comes around the table to give Ilmi a rather enthusiastic hug. "Thanks, Ilmi!"

Ilmi returns the hug and then looks to Toreval with a curious glint in their eyes. "Can I assume you're going to be working on whatever it is you needed to dress like that for again?"

"Possibly," Toreval admits, absently tearing a bit more off of their pastry and gently dipping it into their tea. "I don't suppose you'd mind if I held onto your sash for a while longer?"

Ilmi sighs. "Go ahead—If you're going to be off conspiring and out of your robes, you might as well be wearing the right colors at least." They ruffle Taldee's hair fondly and look back down to them. "I'll add 'make sure Nida doesn't get themself into too much trouble' to your assignment for tomorrow, then, Taldee. Okay?"

"Okay!" Taldee giggles.

Toreval rolls their eyes in amusement. "Stars, kittens, you're worse than the other Elders sometimes..."

"That's because *we* know you better than anyone." Ilmi smirks and affectionately wraps the end of their tail around the closer of Toreval's lower arms. "Whatever you're up to, I know you'll explain it to me eventually—I make no promises about whether I'll be *happy* about it, though."

Toreval stands and gathers both of their kittens into a hug. Their family might be small—and smaller than ever, now—but they couldn't be happier to be part of it.

"Now, Taldee, don't get too far ahead!" Toreval calls, "and stay where we can see you!"

"I will!" Taldee continues scampering ahead down the fern-lined path between the City Arboretum's main building and the smaller glass-walled Conservatory that lies deeper into the trees, although they do seem to be making an attempt to slow down.

It's turned into a lovely morning for a walk in City-on-the-River's nature preserve. The suns haven't quite crested the cliffs yet, as early as it is in the day, and the jungle air is still shrouded in a fine mist. Tree-dwelling cousins of the skimmer-lizards on the river busily flutter after the myriad of jewel-colored insects that are hard at work pollinating all of the blooms from the feather-fruit trees. Their clicks and whistles carry on the soft breeze like one great symphony of interconnected melodies, all underlaid by the sounds of the waterfalls in the distance and the gurgle of the little streams that run down from the lower jungle to join the river as it winds through the city.

"Thank you again for bringing me," says the Ensign walking beside Toreval. He's dressed far more casually today, although still in lightweight versions of his Fleet-issue ivory shirt and dark green trousers. He's rolled up the sleeves of the shirt and has several of its upper buttons undone.

"It's my pleasure, Li," Toreval replies. "As I told you, it's not often I have the chance to take a visitor around to see the sights."

"So you said." The Ensign smiles, gesturing vaguely up the path to where Taldee is impatiently waiting for the two of them. "And the lightning-ball is good company too. I swear, if you could bottle that kid's energy..."

Toreval laughs. "Lapis could rival the stars themselves, some days, yes."

The two of them catch up to Taldee just before they reach the Conservatory. Its tall geodesic domed structure is made mostly out of glass, with support bars between the glass panels of the same sort of shimmering white polycrete material that makes up the smooth domed roofs of the rest of the city. From the outside, only the shadowy form of the interior balcony walkways on the upper levels of the three-story building can be seen among the myriad of brightly purple, black, and occasionally green foliage within. It's a smaller version of the three grand wings of the main Arboretum building itself, although that has parts of its roof open to the sky instead of being one continuous dome.

Taldee is practically bouncing by the time they get there.

"This is the *best* place in the whole Arboretum, Hsu Li!" Taldee takes the Ensign's hand in one of their upper ones impulsively. "All of the shiny flowers from other parts of the Sanctuary live here—you like flowers, right?"

"I do," says the Ensign, allowing himself to be led through the tall glass doors. Toreval has the impression that he's not normally the sort of human to casually touch people the way their species does, but he seems to have no problem letting Taldee hold his hand and lead him around to marvel at all of the plants.

Toreval makes a note in the back of their mind to ask him about this later, just to be sure.

The three of them spend quite some time exploring the Conservatory. Taldee has come here often enough with Toreval and their older siblings that they can name most of the more interesting plants. The kitten proves *more* than delighted to tell the Ensign what each one they recognize is and where on their home planet it comes from.

"Oh!" Taldee stops in front of a cluster of lilac-fronded shrubs on the conservatory's lower level. "These are neat, Hsu Li! Look!"

The Ensign looks the plant over appreciatively. "Very pretty. What are they, then, Lapis?"

"Spikeberry bushes!" Taldee looks up at him and Toreval with an adorably authoritative swish of their tail. "They're what makes my favorite fruit—like the ice-strings we had yesterday."

"Ah, is that so?" Li makes a good show of looking more closely at the tiny green flowers that are just beginning to open on the stems of the small shrubs. "A fine plant indeed, if it produces a tasty fruit like that."

"Yep!" Taldee's tail is still swishing happily. "My Ai-Nida has them in their garden, too, that *their* Ai-Nida planted—but they live out at City-by-the-Mountain. Spikeberries don't like being in really wet places like here, so we can't grow any ourselves..."

"Your Ai-Nida?" The Ensign asks, looking up to Toreval.

"Their grandparent," Toreval answers, simply. It's been a long time since they've seen those particular gardens, themself, since they usually only see their parent at the occasional Council meeting. The last time they went out for a proper visit was years ago, just after Taldee reached an age where they were walking for themself more than being carried. Ilmi's taken the younger kitten out to spend time there more recently, although not since the news of their littermates' deaths arrived.

Toreval remembers their parent's garden fondly, although they would have to admit it was never a place they truly considered their *home*. They spent far too much of their kittenhood here at City-on-the-River for that.

"Ah." The Ensign nods. "Sounds a bit like my own family's home back at Luyten's Star. My Aunties always said you could read the family tree in what bits of the house and gardens different people had added on."

Luyten's Star, Toreval knows, is the nearest of the four 'Major Colonies' to Procyon, sitting only a touch over a single light-year away. As such, it was quite naturally the first to send an expedition of any sort towards their people's Sanctuary—and remains the one with the closest ties to the Florivan people. There's even a small settlement of Florivans there now, including twelve of the Elders who the Council has just sent word to of the need to return to Procyon for the full session where a decision about the Admiral's proposals will be made.

Toreval had visited the system a few times while they were an apprentice to the Nav/Quan team of the starship LSS *Caleana Major*. They remember the main inhabited planet being quite lovely, although they never had a chance to explore much further than the Florivan Sanctuary at North City. They hadn't realized that the Ensign had been raised as one of their people's closest neighbors, but now that he's mentioned it, that fact *does* explain the traces of a distinctive lilting accent in his voice.

Taldee looks up at him wide-eyed. "Are you related to the last Beacon, Hsu Li? She was from Luyten's Star too!"

"The last Beacon?"

"The first human Astral Navigator," Toreval supplies. "I'd assume you're familiar with the story, considering how much longer the people of your home colony have been in contact with us compared to the rest of the human systems."

"Ah, I am—although I'd never heard her called that before." The Ensign nods lightly once again. "I remember studying her and the rest of *Hulthemia's* crew in school." He looks back down to Taldee. "We're not closely related as far as I know, but considering that *everyone* whose ancestors were on the *North* sooner or later shares a few of them, it's not a stretch to think we might have some distant cousins in common."

Taldee silently considers this for a few moments before their ears twitch excitedly. "That counts! It's just like how everyone who's not one of my entiles or siblings is one of *my* cousins."

The Ensign chuckles. "I suppose that makes sense, Lapis. Miss Lin and I wouldn't be particularly *close* cousins, of course."

This does nothing to dissuade Taldee's excitement. "What's it like at Luyten Prime, then? Are there *really* walls and shield-bubbles around all of the houses and things?"

"There are, most places—it keeps the wildlife from deciding to come in and see what folks taste like." The Ensign looks around the Conservatory, shaking his head ever so slightly. "Or the plants, for that matter. The plants back home aren't quite as... *docile*... as the ones you have here. Some of them try to wander into houses too, if you're not careful."

Taldee is all wide-eyed amazement. Toreval can't help being amused—and, to a certain extent, reminded of why *they* had to have a human chaperon accompany them everywhere they went on the occasions when they visited the Ensign's homeworld.

Taldee looks up to them now. "Can I go see wandering plants someday?"

"When you're a bit older, Lapis." Toreval ruffles the kitten's hair with one of their lower hands for a moment. "And *taller*. From what I remember, the Wandering Sagebrush tends to be a bit bigger than Jade and I are—one of those could swallow you up right now, if you got too close to it."

"We had a species of Walking Ferns too, on our island," the Ensign adds. "They're only really in the tropical regions, but they stalk smaller creatures for *days* sometimes before snaring them."

Taldee, once again, has all three eyes wide with delighted curiosity. "Can you keep one of those as a pet? They sound neat!"

The Ensign stifles a laugh. "I had a friend who tried, once... his mother made him send it back out into the forest after it stole too many eggs from her chickens."

Toreval finds themself giggling as well. The most inhabited planet at Luyten's Star is well-known for having a wondrously animate collection of plants and highly armored animals. They have a feeling now that they'll someday need to warn Taldee's eventual spacefaring mentor about keeping them adequately supervised the first time they're allowed to visit its surface. Knowing their youngest kitten as they do, Toreval has no doubt that Taldee *would* get into all sorts of trouble trying to tame one of the smaller carnivorous plants.

"Why did the walking fern want *eggs*?" Taldee asks, tilting their head lightly to one side.

"I'm not really sure—I think it's to do with the mineral content of the shells, actually?" The Ensign shrugs.

"Why don't you sit here and look up some information about Walking Ferns and other animate plants while Li and I refill all of our water bottles?" Toreval gestures to a nearby bench with one lower hand and fishes Taldee's datapad out of the small backpack they're wearing with the upper two. They offer it to their kitten with an encouraging smile. "Then you tell me more about them while we have lunch."

Taldee nods enthusiastically and takes the little device, scampering over to the bench and taking a seat. Within moments, all three of their eyes are intently focused on the display and whatever they're reading. The silver tuft at the end of their long prehensile tail dances with interest.

Toreval smiles at their kitten, then gestures to a nearby alcove. "The refreshment station is this way."

The Ensign follows them, casting an amused glance back at Taldee. The part of his long high-looped ponytail that hangs down swishes softly as he turns his gaze back to Toreval.

"I hope they're not too much for you," Toreval says softly while they're waiting for the drink dispenser to fill the first water bottle. "I did *try* to tell Lapis this morning that they needed to be on their best behavior when showing guests around."

"Oh, it's fine, Celadon, really. They remind me a bit of some of my *actual* cousins—never had any sibs, myself, but the cousins are *many* and they're all younger than me." The Ensign lets out a small laugh. "I can see why this older sibling of Lapis' needed the day off from them to get anything done, that's for sure."

Toreval's ear twitches with amusement. That had, of course, been the extent of their explanation as to why Taldee is with them—their personal desire to see if the kitten's presence would encourage the young human to be more talkative is something they hadn't even mentioned to Ilmi.

"Considering how near we are to the River Festival, I may be bringing Lapis along for a few more days to give Jade more time to themself."

"You mentioned the Festival before…" The Ensign looks to them curiously. "I meant to ask earlier, Celadon. Is that something visitors are allowed to attend?"

Toreval nods and switches the full water bottle out for one of the empty ones. "Of course! We *encourage* visitors to take part in the festivities, even. If you're interested in learning more about our culture and traditions, that's something you won't want to miss."

"From what little I've heard about it, I'm sure I'll enjoy the experience." Li leans against the wall, looking out at the plants in the Conservatory. "What all goes on with it, then?"

"Oh, the usual festival things—music, dancing, little games for the kittens, that sort of thing. All of the different households in the City bring food to share, too, and the Star-Keepers present performances from the story cycles that are about the River and our history. We suspend a translucent stage from the twin bridges just downstream of the falls for them so everyone can see."

"That sounds amazing." The Ensign accepts his refilled water bottle from them and taking a small sip. "You'll have to tell me where to sit for a good view."

"I'll be sure to." Toreval smiles.

They're already trying to think through how they might be able to spend an hour or two of the week-long festival in their disguise so they can see what the Ensign thinks of their home's biggest celebration of the year firsthand. Considering their position as the Council's

Youngest, though, they're not *entirely* sure if that'd be possible just yet.

Once the water bottles are all filled, Toreval and the Ensign go back to the bench to collect Taldee. As expected, the kitten is right where they were left, still raptly attentive to whatever information they've found.

"Learn anything interesting, Lapis?" Toreval asks, offering their kitten their water bottle.

Taldee takes it with their upper hands, since their lower two are still occupied with holding their datapad and stylus. They take a sip, and then nod with an excited swish of their tail. "I did! Walking Ferns are *neat*! Did you know that they move by controlling the flow of water in their roots? They can even open and close their fronds in response to stimuli like being touched or having a tasty bug fly nearby!"

"Fascinating, dear." Toreval lightly pats their kitten on the head. "I don't think I knew about how it was that they seem to walk, although I'd heard the part about them reaching out to grab insects."

"I found a neat film about the ones on Gilmore's Island," Taldee continues, looking up to the Ensign. "Have you ever been there, Hsu Li?"

"Once, on a school trip—we were there when they were migrating west for the monsoon season and the blue snappers were following them." The Ensign chuckles softly, shaking his head. "Home's a funny sort of a place, as far as inhabited planets go. Even our native herbivores are a bit touchy and predatory. We got *so* many lectures about keeping our distance from both sorts of herds while we were there we made a game out of parroting them back to our teachers."

Taldee seems incredibly impressed by this. "Do you want to finish watching the film with me? It still has a bit to go and I think they're going to talk about the evolutionary biology of the stationary plants that share the walking fern's habitat next!"

"Maybe later, Lapis," Toreval gently chides, gesturing down towards the other end of the Conservatory with their tail. "We did promise Li that we'd show him the orchids, remember?"

Taldee seems disappointed only for a moment as they put their datapad back into Toreval's backpack, but then they brighten and swish their tail with their usual excitement once again. They take hold of both Toreval's and the Ensign's hands and pull the two of them in the same direction Toreval had pointed.

"Right! The orchids are *really* neat!" Taldee bounces happily as they walk. "You did say you like orchids, right, Hsu Li?"

"I do at that." The Ensign chuckles, sharing a glance with Toreval that they take to mean that he's *thoroughly* amused by their kitten. "I grow them as a hobby, actually—my grandmother got me started with some cuttings off of the wind orchids one of our ancestors brought with them on the *North*."

"Wind orchids?" Toreval asks. "What sort are those?"

"They're a sort of mounding plant with spiky leaves that have white flowers with long spurs when they bloom." The Ensign makes a vague gesture with his free hand. There's a pleasingly animated excitement to the edges of his tone as he speaks, not unlike a subtler version of Lapis' eager tail-waving when reporting about something new that's sparked their interest. Toreval finds it more endearing than they expected. "Traditionally they're grown just as much for the beauty of the foliage as for the blossoms, and they come in all sorts of different leaf patterns and blossom sizes. The main one I take care of is just a standard *Vanda falcata*. I'll show you a picture once we get wherever Lapis is taking us, if you like."

Toreval nods. "I would like to see that, yes."

"They sound neat!" Taldee chimes in.

"They are." The Ensign smiles softly. "You should see the collection my grandmother had. Practically every room in her house had at least one wind orchid somewhere."

"That sounds like Jade!" Taldee giggles, pulling the two of them the final few steps and through the curtains into the Conservatory's orchid room. "They have comet orchids in the windows in our nest room and their workroom."

Toreval stifles a giggle themself. Taldee's right about their sibling's fondness for the sweet-smelling blossoms of the native comet orchid. They can't help wondering if Ilmi *would* get along with this human if the two of them met, but at the same time they have a feeling that forcing such a meeting would only upset Ilmi. Their plan, after all, is just to get to know the Ensign—not to use him as a means to remind their sweet eldest kitten that humans are their people's *friends* for a reason.

"Comet orchids?" the Ensign asks, echoing Toreval's earlier tone, but unable to mimic the curious flicking gesture they'd made with their ears.

"These!" Taldee lets go of Toreval's hand to better pull the Ensign to the corner of the room where the Conservatory's collection of their sibling's favorite flowers are sitting.

Each mass of spear-like black and tan-streaked foliage is neatly tucked into a mound of moss sitting like an island on a flat dish with its long cream-colored roots winding in and out. Two of the larger plants have tall bloom-spikes just beginning to unfurl their brilliantly amber blossoms, while a smaller one is already in full bloom. Each six-petaled cupped-star blossom bears a long tail-like spur coming down from the back of it, where the flower's nectar is housed.

The Ensign laughs brightly when he sees the plants. "Oh, I can see why your sibling likes them!" He makes an appreciative gesture and looks to Toreval. "Imagine this, but *green* and with white blossoms that are a bit daintier, and *that's* pretty much what a wind orchid looks like."

"Is that so?" Toreval comes over to join him and Taldee. They're fond of comet orchids themself, too, ever since their three eldest kittens first presented them with one as a gift because it matched the color of their then-newly-donned Elder's robes. That particular comet orchid is the one that Ilmi now takes care of for them which lives in their family's nest chamber.

"Yes, see?" Li pulls out his pocket-com and shows them and Taldee a picture of a surprisingly similar plant in the colors he'd described, although with the mound of moss holding its roots perched atop a stately white ceramic pot. "This is one of mine."

"They do look quite similar." Toreval nods appreciatively. "What do you think, Lapis?"

Taldee looks between the image on the Ensign's projected holoscreen and the comet orchids in front of them. Their tail waves happily. "It's like they're cousins! Do yours smell as nice as these?"

"They do, although with more of a vanilla sort of scent than these." The Ensign leans over towards the amber-tinged yellow blossoms of one of the smaller comet orchids. "This is more like cinnamon and mint, I think."

Taldee mimics him, then tugs on his hand and gestures towards a different corner of the glass-walled room. "You should come smell the green purse ones! They're blooming too—Jade always says they smell like bread."

"Oh, really?" The Ensign tilts his head curiously. "Well, then! Lead the way, Lapis."

Toreval can't help smiling at the sight of their youngest kitten and the Ensign wandering around the orchid room and stopping at each flower to comment on its smells and colors and compare it to pictures of the Earth-origin orchids Li knows. They're glad to see that both he and Taldee are having fun with this little excursion.

They've not been able to find out much about his thoughts on the Admiral he serves or the War his people have been brought into yet, unfortunately. Still, Toreval knows that today's goal is more to get to know the young human better and to encourage him to be more comfortable with them. They're sure that once they've achieved some degree of rapport with him, the Ensign will be willing to be candid with them and provide the insight they need in order to make the decisions they need to make.

Toreval has to admit, too, that they're enjoying themself. How long has it been since they were free to take a day like this and wander without having to maintain their carefully-crafted Elder's composure?

How long, too, has it been since they came to visit the City Arboretum's Conservatory at all? It takes Toreval a moment to come up with the answer to that question, and it's bittersweet when they find it. Inayan had been interested in botany long before they chose the Ranger's path; they'd assisted in *Caleana Major*'s hydroponics bay, too, when they and their littermates were still apprentices. The last time they visited, when they and Iralee brought their counterparts home to meet Toreval and the rest of the family: *that* was the last time Toreval had come here.

Toreval sighs, leaning over to take in the smell of the comet orchids for themself. None of these were in bloom when Inayan and Iralee were here, but the sweet-custard tree in the center of the main section of the Conservatory was. Inayan had always been fond of that tree, even as a kitten. Toreval lost count of the times they'd had to climb up it to retrieve them and Iralee, back when their first litter was still so young that they hadn't even been presented to the Council to receive their public names. Ilmi, of course, had always preferred to wait patiently on the ground by the glass ferns for the rest of the family to come back down.

That was all so long ago.

Toreval's soul aches for those days, and for any days when their little family was whole. They'd been so young themself when they became a parent—*far* too young—but their kittens were and are their world. Letting them leave for the stars was hard enough, but to know now that two of them will never come home? Toreval isn't sure they'll ever fully come to terms with that.

Toreval is only able to brood on such things for a few minutes. Soon, Taldee has noticed that they're still standing beside the comet orchids and scampers over to retrieve them.

"Nida! Come see! This one smells just like honey-ash cakes, but Hsu Li doesn't believe me." Taldee looks up at them with wide, eager eyes. "He's never *had* honey-ash cakes. Did you know that?"

Toreval lets their youngest kitten take them by one of their lower hands. They smile softly, letting their mind focus once more on the here and now. "Really, now? Well, I think I know what we're getting for our snack once we're done here..."

ON A RATHER SUNNY MORNING A FEW DAYS after their excursion to the City Arboretum with Taldee and the Ensign, Toreval is once again up in the Council House rafters.

This time, though, it's in their usual place up above the smaller meeting hall that is used for discussing the everyday business of the Council. As the Youngest among their people's Elders, Toreval is one of the two people whose presence is required at all meetings—but there's no rule that says they have to stay on the ground. They do more listening than talking most of the time anyway, and they're certainly still not interested in participating in the circular arguments about the Admiral's proposals that have been re-emerging every time one of the Elders who lives in one of the Sanctuary's other cities arrives.

At the moment, they have their ears trained down on the handful of Elders below them who have finally moved on to discussing the last bits of planning and set-up required for the opening night of the week-long River Festival which starts tomorrow. While it's the final item on the to-do list for this morning's meeting and something that *does* interest Toreval, they're still not directly involved with the matter, so they're only partly paying attention. Their eyes, instead, are focused on the dimmed-down holoscreen in their hands and the message that has just arrived from one of their small number of close friends who've left for the stars over the years.

Navy Irleeim had been fresh out of their apprenticeship and undergoing training from one of their people's experts on mental health and wellness when Toreval was a kitten, and had often been the one kitten-sitting for them and Laryven and Liret before they were old enough to begin being properly educated. When Toreval joined *Caleana Major*'s crew as Elder Azul's apprentice, Navy was there, too, as a passenger bound for Earth and the Sol Central Academy of Medicine's Psychology program. The two of them had gotten to be good friends during the journey and have maintained a close correspondence ever since. Now, as a civilian consultant who works with the various research and development programs at the Shipyards at Teegarden's Star—including the Defense Fleet's small craft test pilot program—Navy is in a unique position to give an opinion about the War and their people's potential involvement.

Toreval reads through the message. After the initial greetings and inquiries of how they and their kittens are faring, they come to the part that matters most at the moment:

> Well, Celadon, what can I say? Nida did send me a note about the full Council being called in, and they asked some of the same questions you did, so there's no need to bother with trying to be subtle about it. Admiral Marvin's spoken to me a time or two about the possibilities of our involvement as well, of course, since I've been the only Florivan on hand here before the Rangers picked her up to take her to Procyon to talk to all of you.
>
> As far as whether our human friends are capable of defending themselves? They're trying. Considering what I've heard about the situation, though, I'm not sure that flocks of tiny single-person fighter craft waiting around each of the Coalition's systems to meet the eventual invaders is going to be enough. I'm no strategist, but even I can see how easily they'll be overwhelmed. It won't be a good situation for anyone's morale, I can tell you that.
>
> I'm also not sure how well sending squadrons of the same sort of fighters off to be posted on T'irsh-fel and Prelvee ships at the battlefronts is going to work for them. The environmental extremes those pilots

will have to deal with alone is going to be a problem. I've visited both kinds of ships; the choice is between the kind of humid cold that'll freeze your ears off if you're not careful, even if you're wearing ice gear, and something that's a bit like the height of summer where you are but with nearly twice the gravity. I'd take the warmth of the Prelvee ship if I had to choose, but neither is particularly pleasant to spend very long in. Any group of humans serving on their 'expeditionary force' will be stressed by their living situation for sure; the fact that the Alliance's best plan is to use these humans as a direct counter to the Novan's battle strategies? Even the human psychologists I've been consulting with aren't too confident about that.

Then again, as I've told you before, the pilots I've been working with from the day I got here in their test pilot program are the sort of humans who seem to have very little sense of self-preservation whatsoever to begin with. You'd like them, I think. They all have to come see me once a month, or whenever they happen to be injured and need to be cleared to fly again. I see some of them once a week, because of that! The new pilots that are being trained and organized into the Darter squadrons are mostly the same: thrill-seekers with a strong sense of duty and enough eccentricity and natural aptitude for thinking through three-dimensional space that I'm sure quite a few of them would have made fine Navigators.

It's such a very human thing to be relying on these people to put up what's essentially a last stand in the face of overwhelming odds—and even to have thought it was a viable plan to use occupied small-craft like this in the first place. I don't think there's another species in the galaxy that would have come up with this nonsense.

I will admit that I'm worried, Celadon.

The T'irsh-fel and Prelvee liaisons who've visited the shipyards often make time to speak to me, and they've been quite frank about what these Novans are like. I'm not sure that their Imperium's conquering forces have more than a cursory respect for the Greater Galactic Powers' listings of non-combatant and protected species, especially if they get close enough into our systems to attack civilian vessels like they did T3V *Simone* when they first showed up. I don't know if they can be expected to return jumpers from those ships if they do capture them—stars forbid—and it certainly doesn't seem likely to me that any species whose way is never-ending conquest wouldn't want to try to use us if they ever found out the truth of the Drive.

I don't doubt that you've already considered all of this. I know Nida has, and I'll tell you the same thing I told them when they asked me: I *don't* think we're safe. I don't think we can *be* safe when our human friends are threatened. If our goal is to integrate our societies and share the stars with them, how can we leave them to face this without us even if we *were* safe? I'm grateful I'm in a position to help as a civilian, even if all I can do is try to keep these pilots reasonably sane.

Needless to say, I'm keen to hear what the Council decides about all of this. Don't expect me to leave my post either way. I hope *you* at least can understand why I'm here. Nida's still not pleased with it, especially since I still haven't bothered with taking a counterpart to 'protect' me, but for the moment they're not forcing me to be disobedient.

What do you think, then, Celadon?

Which way is the Council's Youngest going to guide them? I wouldn't be surprised if it does come down to you, my friend... I don't envy you at all the stress you must be under.

Toreval sighs softly, looking up into the higher rafters and away from the rest of the letter on their holoscreen. There's so much they've *wanted* to talk to Navy about ever since Iralee and Inayan first came to them with the same concerns, but couldn't because of the secrecy involved in the work their kittens were doing. They still haven't told their friend of anything more than that their kittens were lost while out on Ranger business, same as they've told everyone else here at the Sanctuary. They wish even more now that they could be open with Navy about everything, but once again they find their hands tied by the situation.

Toreval glances down at the meeting below them. Judging by the sound of it, their input is still not required. They tap out a reply that's likely far briefer than Navy would prefer:

```
Navy, my friend, I miss you.

My kittens are well, although both
are still grieving in their own ways.
I still worry for Ilmi, and I know it
would be good for them to talk to you.
Perhaps you could write them? I'm sure
they'll see your counsel as wiser than
my own—in no small part because it is.
(I still maintain you'd be far better
suited to the Elder's role than I ever
will…)

As far as the War: I don't know what
the Council's Youngest thinks yet. I
know how I've felt and still feel, but
I don't know yet if my own regrets are
```

blinding me to what must be done to
keep our people safe. My soul aches
to agree with you, for my kittens'
sake—but perhaps I'm too closely tied
to all of this to be able to think
rationally.

You've said Admiral Marvin talks to
you. What do you think of *her*, then?
I'm still deciding there, myself. (I've
spoken a few times lately to the young
Ensign who serves as her assistant. Do
you know him as well? Taldee's become
quite fond of him.)

As far as the Council's decision: I
can't say I'd agree with you about it
being up to me. The Youngest's role is
to speak only after all have spoken,
and who knows if the Council would
listen to me… but I will do my best.

I'm still seeking out the answers I
need. Thank you for adding your wisdom
to those, old friend. I trust you more
than I trust myself lately.

There's far more that they would write, if they could, or
that they would say if they could speak to Navy in person.
Toreval, though, has once again found themself alone with
their thoughts and the weight of their responsibilities.
They're used to that, but for the first time since they
donned their Elder's robes, they're genuinely feeling *lonely*
in their position. More than that, they're still somewhat at
a loss for what to do.

Toreval's musings are interrupted by the sound of a voice calling up to them.

"You can come down, now, dear, they're all gone."

Toreval stows their pocket-com away and drops from their perch in the rafters as an elegant flutter of amber silks. They land with a practiced polish at the side of the Eldest's seat at the head of the conference table.

The Eldest smiles softly at them and twitches their ears with amusement. "If *I* could still get away with lurking up above during these endless meetings so no one could tell how much attention I was paying..."

Toreval stifles a chuckle. "I promise I *was* listening, Eldest."

"I'm sure you were, dear." The Eldest arches their eyebrows. "I only had to call to you twice this time."

"You did? I didn't hear..."

"I did notice that." All three of the Eldest's eyes soften. "Don't worry, dear, the others weren't here to notice themselves."

Toreval barely manages to hold back a sigh. "Thank you."

The Eldest stands from their chair now, resting both dark grey-blue lower hands lightly on the head of their ornately-carved wooden cane. The white silks of their robes rustle softly as they gesture with one of the upper pair. "Lost in thought, then?"

"...Something like that," Toreval admits.

The Eldest reaches up with their upper hands now and gently straightens the folds of Toreval's veils from where their landing had jostled them out of position. "I'm not surprised. You have much on your mind these days, don't you, dear?" Their voice is just as soothing and gentle now as Toreval remembers it being when they were a small kitten.

Toreval nods lightly. "More than I'd like to have."

"I know." The Eldest lets one of their hands linger as a reassuring squeeze of Toreval's shoulder for a moment, then gestures towards the door leading to the balcony that encircles this level of the Council House. "Come, dear, walk with me for a bit? You know I'm always here to listen if you need me—and if not, you can listen to *me* ramble for a bit before you leave for the afternoon."

"Thank you, Eldest. I'd like that." Toreval lets the older Florivan take hold of one of their own upper arms and walks with them out onto the balcony. They don't know how the Eldest always seems to know just how to set them at ease—but then, no one knows Toreval better, not even their own parent. Even though they're well past old enough to understand the truth now, Toreval's kittenhood imprint on this Elder who took them in even before their eyes had opened and raised them until their actual parent was well enough to take care of them again has never gone away. The one thing that gave Toreval stability, too, when they first returned to Procyon as an *exceedingly* young parent and future member of the Council, was that being "re-apprenticed" to the Eldest let them return to the side of the person whom they had never wanted to leave as a kitten.

The two of them have only barely reached the first archway when the Eldest speaks again. "I *have* been meaning to ask how your..." They pause, taking on an almost teasing tone as they look down to Toreval. "Hmm.

Shall we call it an *unofficial* assignment? I'm curious to know how that has been going."

Toreval finds their tail swishing with embarrassment. "You're... aware of that, Eldest?"

"Now really, dear. Don't you know by now that I'm aware of just about *everything*?" The Eldest laughs brightly and gives Toreval a knowingly amused look with their third eye. "There's a few people who've mentioned it to me—particularly your cousin Taivin."

"Oh." Toreval sighs. It's only natural that Indigo would say something to the Eldest; the two of them are good friends, after all, and Indigo probably assumed that the Eldest was already aware of what Toreval was doing.

"Don't worry, dear, I'm not aiming to stop you." The Eldest gives Toreval's arm a gentle pat with their free upper hand. "I think it's nice that you're taking some time for yourself for once outside the Council House."

"That's not *exactly* what I was intending, Eldest... I'm only trying to gather more information to prepare for the discussions of the Admiral's proposal. That's all."

"Oh, of course, dear." The subtle twitch of the Eldest's ears gives Toreval the impression that they don't entirely believe it. "But still, you're enjoying the time you've been spending with the Ensign?"

"Well..." Toreval turns their eyes out towards the purple and black foliage of the trees and the crisp white domes of their city. They weren't expecting to be asked about any of this. "Ensign Hsu is pleasant company," they say, settling on as neutral of an answer and tone as they can come up with. "I suppose I have to admit that it's been a nice change of pace, showing him the city."

"I see." The Eldest seems to stifle a chuckle. "And setting your robes aside allows you to be yourself with him?"

"It... Well." Toreval flushes, looking back to the kind eyes of their almost-parent. They don't want to admit how true those words really are. "I chose to disguise myself so that he would be more candid with me, Eldest. I know the humans who've come to speak with the Council before always tend to be more guarded around Elders."

"Is that so?" The Eldest smiles again, stopping now to stand by the balcony railing and look out at the river and the city spreading along its banks. "Well, then, dear, I see you've thought that through, at least. It's not *traditional*, but I don't see a reason to interfere with it."

Toreval lets out a small sigh of relief. "Thank you, Eldest."

A long moment passes, the two of them watching the distant motion of their people through the city's streets and courtyards and out where preparations are being made for the festival that will soon be held on the river. Toreval's thoughts are more distant still, caught up as they have been for a long time now between the stars and the Sanctuary and the war that threatens them all. Navy's words and the impassioned pleas of their now-lost kittens echo in their mind as one.

"Toreval?" asks the Eldest at last, gently, pulling them out of the maelstrom of their thoughts.

"Hmm?" Toreval looks over to them, once again embarrassed. "Forgive me, Eldest, my mind was... elsewhere. Did you say something?"

"No, dear, it's all right." The Eldest lightly sets a hand on Toreval's shoulder. They're quiet for a moment longer, and then they chuckle. "You know, when I first met you, you were the *smallest* newly-caught kitten I'd ever seen? And the fluffiest, too—right down to your tail!"

"You've said," Toreval replies, unable to help smiling. They've seen the pictures from when their eyes first opened, and they were still so much of a little silver fluffy thing that their ears and limbs were hard to discern out of all of their kitten-fur.

"And somehow, I knew even then that you'd be the sort of kitten who got into everything..." The Eldest gives them a knowing but affectionate look. "And I was right. You've turned out to be the *best* sort of trouble-making scamp, dear—a kitten after my own heart if there ever was one."

"Thank you, Eldest." Toreval stifles a giggle. Considering the near-unbelievable stories they've heard from the Eldest's own youth, they know that's meant as a compliment. The sentiment warms their soul, too, especially the part of them that has never forgotten that there was a time when they didn't know that they had someone else to call their Nida at all.

"I know you have other reasons for this latest little scheme of yours," the Eldest continues, "but it's good to see you've found some happiness in it too. With all you've been through, it's about time."

Toreval doesn't know what to say to that. They absently straighten out a few wrinkles from the layers of silks in their robes. "I... I'm glad you think so, Eldest."

The Eldest gives Toreval's shoulder another gentle pat. "I'd like to meet him eventually, you know. Outside the Admiral's business."

"Eldest?" Toreval tilts their head, confused.

"Your Ensign."

"Li isn't *mine...*" Toreval starts to say.

"Of course, dear." The Eldest's ears twitch with something resembling amusement. "But any friend of yours is someone I'd like to know better myself."

"Ah." Toreval hesitates, although they don't know why. "I think you'd like him—Taldee does, at any rate..."

"And you find his company 'pleasant.'" The Eldest smiles to them with a genial nod. "I'll find an opportunity sooner or later—although unlike *someone* I know, I'm not particularly in a position to change clothes and call it a disguise."

Toreval can't stifle their giggles this time. "Is there anyone *alive* who's ever seen you in public without the silks, Eldest?"

Toreval's ears catch the sound of footsteps behind them just in time that the voice cutting in to the conversation doesn't surprise them.

"*I* have, Elder Celadon, although that was a *long* time ago for both of us..." The deep blue Elder who is now approaching from a nearby doorway laughs. Unlike Toreval and the Eldest, this Elder isn't in their formal robes. Instead, they're in a charcoal-grey civilian space service uniform with ruby-toned silk ribbons woven through the twin braided hair buns at the back of their head. Toreval knows them well; Elder Caeruleus is one of the handful of spacefaring Elders the Council has been waiting for. "I think they were still pulling stunts as the Youngest at the time, too, just like you do."

"Oh, now, little sibling, don't go embarrassing me in front of the kittens." The Eldest laughs too, meeting Elder Caeruleus with a warm hug. "It's good to see you, though—and speaking of *kittens*..."

Just as the Eldest says this, two familiar adolescents not much older than Taldee bounce out of the same doorway, both of them dressed in white tunics. The taller of the two is a deep greenish-blue under their stripes, while the shorter is a more grey-toned version of the same color, similar to the Eldest. They're followed by a middle-aged human man with a deeply tan complexion and geometric tattoos peeking out from the bald portion of his head of close-cropped dark hair.

"Nida!" the two kittens call as one, scampering over to give their parent an enthusiastic hug. The Eldest happily sets their cane aside to wrap both of them up in their silk-draped arms.

"Marbree, Myrval, oh *stars* how the two of you have grown..." Each of the Eldest's upper hands settles on one of the two kittens' heads in turn and ruffles their ears.

"We've only been gone for three months, Nida," little River Myrval says, looking up with wide, curious eyes. "*Marbree* grew."

Toreval lets out a small laugh at that. Myrval is a survivor-smallest kitten, like Ilmi—and like Ilmi did, they're going through that stage where they're very aware of how much faster their littermate is developing. They and Ocean Marbree are fully three years older than Taldee, but anyone who didn't know the three of them would assume Myrval was at least a year younger if not more.

"I did!" Marbree giggles. "Uncle Joseph says I'm going to be *tall* someday, Nida, like you!"

"You think so, Joseph?" the Eldest asks, looking over to Elder Caeruleus' Navigator with an amused sparkle in all three of their eyes.

"I wouldn't be surprised, Eldest," says the man, giving a polite bow of his head in greeting. "Most of your kittens turn out that way."

"*Some* of us don't," says Myrval, looking up and noticing Toreval's presence now. Their tail waves excitedly. "Like you!" They scamper over to give Toreval a greeting hug as well.

"Did you miss us, Celadon?" Marbree now comes over to join the hug. They really *have* grown; they're nearly at eye level with Toreval's upper shoulders now. Myrval is no less than a head shorter.

Toreval ruffles each kitten's hair briefly. "Of course I did. Lapis did too—I'm sure they'll be happy the two of you are home in time for the River festival."

"*I'm* happy we're home for the festival," says Marbree, excitement coloring their tone. "It means we don't have to miss Nida's plum scones and the water games!"

Myrval nods in agreement before leaving Toreval to hug onto their parent's legs once more.

Elder Caeruleus stifles a laugh, lightly nudging their Navigator with one of their lower elbows. "The kittens aren't the only ones who were keen on us getting *Deinocheirus* here in time for all of that, if we had to come home ahead of schedule. I could have *sworn* someone was insisting on giving us points for double-jumps the whole way…"

The Eldest looks to the human as well, twitching their ears with amusement. "Is that so, Joseph?"

"What can I say, Eldest?" he quips, absently cracking his knuckles. "I never could resist the offer of your fine planet's hospitality—and as for who *asked* for those points…" The Navigator shoots his counterpart a brief, affectionately teasing smirk. "Well, we're here, at any rate."

"That you are." The Eldest retrieves their cane with their tail and rests their lower hands on it once more. "And it's good to have all of you home, even with circumstances being what they are."

Elder Caeruleus nods. "It is." They look to Toreval now, tilting their head curiously. "What's this I hear about you being up to mischief again?"

Toreval awkwardly smooths some wrinkles out of their robes. They hadn't expected any of the other Elders to be aware of their doings at all, much less the ones who are coming in from the stars. "I wouldn't call it *mischief*…"

Elder Caeruleus raises their third eyebrow, then looks to the Eldest. "You'll tell me when you catch me up on the rest of the Council business after we feed these bottomless pits you call your kittens?"

"Naturally." The Eldest smiles serenely and reaches over to pat Toreval on the shoulder. "Are you joining us, dear, or did you have plans with your 'research subject'?"

Toreval finds themself feeling like they're a kitten again, being asked where they'd stashed some borrowed shiny thing or other that needs to be returned. Their tail swishes subtly under the layers of their robes with a hesitant embarrassment. "I... Well, yes, actually, Eldest."

The Eldest and Elder Caeruleus share an amused look.

Little Myrval looks up to Toreval with a disappointed droop of their ears. "Does that mean you *aren't* going to have lunch with us?"

Toreval smiles at them reassuringly. They know all too well who the kitten is really asking after. "I might not be able to, and I know Jade is busy helping prepare the festival stage, but Lapis is assisting Indigo and Monica with their baking this morning. You can tell them I said it's okay for them to spend the rest of the day with you and Ocean."

Marbree's tail swishes with impossible-to-conceal excitement. "Thank you, Celadon!" They look up to the Eldest with the same eager look in all three of their eyes that Myrval is now wearing. "That means we get tea cookies after lunch, right?

"Of course, dear." The Eldest chuckles and holds out one of their upper hands to each kitten, their lower pair still resting on their cane. "Come on, then, let's leave Elder Celadon to their business."

The kittens happily take their hands and walk with them back towards the door.

"We'll talk another time, then," says Elder Caeruleus, nodding to Toreval. "I do look forward to hearing your thoughts on everything, *Youngest*." They put a special emphasis on Toreval's title, but in a polite way that suggests they do think Toreval has something worth saying.

"And I yours," Toreval replies. Elder Caeruleus, after all, was the first among their people ever to become an Elder *after* making their compact with a human Navigator and taking a position as a starship's jumper. The precedent for spacefaring Elders exists because of *them*; if anyone has a clear view of the situation, it would be them.

With a swish of their tail, Elder Caeruleus turns to follow the Eldest and their two apprentices. They rest both of their left hands genially on their Navigator's arm as he escorts them out. He gives Toreval a little wave as the two of them disappear through the doorway.

Toreval smiles, watching them go, then turns back out towards the balcony railing. They rest their upper pair of arms on it and lean there, staring out at the city below and the river that runs through it. They sigh softly after a moment, although they're not sure why. There are too many feelings layered on top of each other inside them for them to be able to identify a single cause.

Whatever the cause, Toreval doesn't have time to linger, so they turn from the view and head back inside. They still have to return home and change into their disguise, after all, and it wouldn't do to keep the Ensign waiting too long. They know he must be waiting for them by now, too, down at the same fountain where they first met.

They've promised to take him down the river to tour one of the more easily-accessible cave formations this afternoon—just the two of them, as well, since poor Taldee has had a fear of going underground ever since they became separated from their siblings during an educational tour as a very small kitten and spent several hours lost there. Toreval still holds out hope that their youngest will grow past that eventually, but they're waiting for Taldee to be old enough to be ready to choose to go into such places again.

Toreval themself likes caves, particularly this one, and they can't deny a small thrill at being able to share it with their young human friend. They can tell themself all they want that they're just getting to know him so that he'll be honest with them when the time comes to ask their questions, but deep down they know that the Eldest is right: they *do* enjoy Li's company.

They never realized before just how much they missed being just *themself* with someone, and it's so natural to be that around him. Toreval, in their disguise, doesn't have to hold themself to the standards of behavior befitting a parent and Elder. They don't have to think about it; Li just lets them be *Toreval*, not 'Elder Celadon, Youngest of the Council'. He doesn't expect anything but their company, and he seems to appreciate spending time with them too.

They know their friendship with Li can only ever be temporary—he'll leave, after all, when the Admiral's business with the council is done, and their place will always be here in the Sanctuary—but Toreval can't help but cherish the experience while it lasts.

Two hours or so later, Toreval and Li have reached the small visitors' center which serves as the access point to the Still-Water Caverns.

"All right, you two, you have the map of all of the public trails on your pocket-coms now, and these—" The young geologist behind the information desk whose saffron-shaded tunic marks them as a member of Elder Azul's household holds out two shimmering purple pendants on long necklace chords. "—Are your location transponders. Put them on, please, and return them to me on your way out."

"What are these for?" Li asks, accepting the transponders. He puts one on, then helpfully drapes the other over Toreval's own head.

"In the event you or your counterpart become misplaced or injured," the young geologist says with a nonchalant shrug, "the transponder will allow us to locate and extract you in a timely fashion."

"Ah." Li nods, then looks to Toreval with a teasing glimmer in his eye. "Well, Celadon here isn't my counterpart... but I'll do my best not to get separated from them anyway."

"Oh?" The young geologist looks to Toreval with a questioning swish of their sky blue tail.

"No, only a friend who happened to be free to show him some of the sights while he's visiting the Sanctuary." Toreval lets out a small laugh. They're far enough from their usual haunts that their disguise is working on other Florivans too, it seems. This is the third time since they got on the small river ferry to come here that someone has made the assumption that Li is their Navigator. It does make sense, in a way; a human visitor who comes here in the company of a single individual rather than as part of a group *would* be more likely to be that individual's counterpart.

"I see." The young geologist makes a genial nod to both of them. "In any case, I hope you enjoy your visit. Do let me know if you have any questions?"

"We will, thank you." Toreval turns to Li, still more amused than not. "Well, Li! Are you ready to see some neat rocks?"

Li chuckles and makes a sweeping gesture towards the archway marking the path down into the caverns. "Of course, Celadon. Lead the way."

Toreval leads their human friend down the winding ramp that has been built into the cave entrance to make the interior easier for visitors to reach. The path is lit on either side by small globe-like lanterns at regular intervals which cast their warm golden light onto the water-hewn walls and gently sloping pebbled floor. After a few minutes of walking, the two of them have reached the first major gallery of the cavern system.

All around them, stalactites stretch down from the high domed ceiling towards their matching stalagmites, many of which are even taller than Li. A steady, gentle dripping echoes in the distance, along with the trickling of the underground stream which flows alongside the path that has been carefully laid out for visitors to walk upon. Tiny crystals glimmer from the surface of the cave walls in the soft light of the lanterns which mark the borders of the path and the places where it forks to follow different trails down into the deeper chambers.

"What do you think?" Toreval asks, breaking the serene silence which had descended upon both of them when they first entered the cave.

"It's lovely." Li pauses to take a sip from the water bottle he's wearing clipped to his belt. "I've not had many chances to come to places like this, but I do enjoy visiting them."

"I've been coming here off and on since I was a kitten, although it's been a while since I had the opportunity." Toreval tilts their head curiously. "You don't have caverns to visit back at Luyten's Star?"

"Not on Prime—the planet's geology isn't right for this sort of cave to even form, from what I remember. Closest thing we had back home were extinct volcanoes and networks of lava tubes, or sea caves around some of the islands, but it's not quite the same thing." Li shrugs, then gets that same teasing glimmer in his eyes once again. "And I'm *hoping* this system isn't inhabited by touchy little predatory lichens, since there wasn't a meter-long list of local life forms to keep one's distance from posted at the entry gate?"

"I see." Toreval stifles a giggle. "And no, just the odd blind fish and flutter-frogs, that's all. Rest assured, neither of *those* are particularly dangerous, and neither are most of the insects and algae they prey on."

"Good to know. I think I like this planet of yours, Celadon." Li flashes them the briefest of grins. "It's nice visiting somewhere where ninety percent of the native life *doesn't* think I'd make a good snack."

"As long as you stay out of their territory and wear the right kinds of parasite repellent when you're outside the Cities," Toreval quips, "that other ten percent shouldn't bother you either."

"I'll keep that in mind." Li pulls out his pocket-com and activates the holoscreen to display the map the young geologist at the information desk gave him. "Which way are we going?"

Toreval points to a particular green-highlighted chamber on the projected image. "You could spend *days* exploring this place, or longer… but the grand crystal room has always been my favorite spot. I'd like to take you there, if you don't mind."

"That sounds promising." Li looks over the map briefly, then slips the deactivated device back into his pocket. He gestures towards one of the lantern-lit openings on the far end of the chamber. "We take that path there, don't we?"

"We do." Toreval starts walking that way. Li follows them.

Toreval falls silent once again as the two of them follow the well-lit path through the caverns. They walk slowly, taking in all of the details of the different rock formations around them. Some are like frozen waterfalls of smooth, glistening stone. Others bear delicate assemblages of minerals clinging onto small crevices like the mosses which grow on the trees and stones on the surface.

Toreval had forgotten how peaceful it can be down here, particularly on a day like this where there are so few other visitors touring the caverns. Their keen catlike ears can pick up the distant strains of other voices, of course, but the majority of the soundscape is simply the soothing trickles and drips of water and the soft sounds of their and Li's footsteps.

It's been a long time since Toreval visited this beautiful, otherworldly place. As with the Arboretum, the last time they came here was with Iralee and their counterpart, Johan. Ilmi and Inayan had stayed in the city that day to have other adventures with Taldee and Inayan's own counterpart, Rick—a brave young Ranger if ever there was one, but one who had disliked the concept of going underground even more than Taldee does.

Iralee was the one among Toreval's kittens who always loved exploring the caves most, of course, and they'd been fortunate enough to find a counterpart who shared that interest. Toreval had spent the whole day in the deeper passages with the two of them and one of Iralee's kittenhood friends who's still a caving guide here, enjoying themself thoroughly even as the four of them were wriggling through the tight spaces between the visitor paths and the parts of the caverns which require permits and safety certifications to explore.

Toreval lets out a small sigh, almost without noticing it escape their lips. They're not sure why they keep bringing Li to all of the places that remind them most of Iralee and Inayan. They weren't aware before now how much they seem to be doing that.

There's no denying that they're still mourning for their kittens—and no doubt in their mind that they will be for the rest of their own life, in some way or another. It hurts in a way they can't even describe to be here walking through the beauty of the flowing rock formations without Iralee by their side to excitedly tell them about the stories each one holds about the region's history. It had hurt that way too, they realize, to go through the vast collection at the Arboretum without Inayan there to similarly gush about the uses of each of the plants. These places live in their memory as Iralee and Inayan's places—just as the Star-Keeper's archive is Ilmi's or the Council House their own.

Toreval aches for there to have been something more they could have done; for some single thing that could have been different so that Iralee and Inayan would have come home to them. No matter how long they think on it, though, they can't find a way they could truly have changed what is—and *that*, perhaps, hurts even more than knowing their kittens are gone in itself. Powerless: that's the word they've been looking for to describe their part in this.

Toreval was the one who *agreed* to allow Iralee and Inayan to go, but how could they not? Their kittens did what they thought was right, and Toreval had never believed in holding them back. Now, though, when all that's left are memories and regrets, all they can do is wander through the places their kittens loved and miss them—and wish that they were here once more.

"Celadon?" Li's voice brings them back into the present, as does the sensation of his hand gently settling on their shoulder. "Is something wrong?"

"Hm?" Toreval stops walking and looks up. "No... why do you ask?"

"Partly your expression..." Li takes on a gentler but pointedly cheerful tone. "And partly the fact that if I'm remembering the map right, I'd say we passed the path that takes us to the grand crystal room about ten minutes ago."

"Oh?" Toreval looks around, then sets one of their upper palms on their face for a moment to hide how embarrassed they are. "So we have. Sorry about that, Li. It's... easy to get lost in thought around here."

"I can see how it would be." The young human flashes them a reassuringly cheeky grin. "I'm glad I said something, then, before you led me clear to the other side of the planet."

Toreval finds themself giggling. "Well, this cave doesn't go *that* far..." They turn and start walking in the correct direction, gesturing with their tail for Li to follow them. "Thank you, though."

"Anytime, Celadon." Li is silent for a moment, then looks to them once more with a hint of concerned curiosity and warmth in his tone. "Is it impolite of me to ask what had you so distracted?"

"It isn't impolite. I..." Toreval turns their third eye to him momentarily as they hesitate. His expression is gentle, and for reasons they don't understand it sets them at ease. They can't help but want to be at least vaguely honest with him. "My household... the family I belong to... we lost two of our younger family members recently. This place reminds me so much of one of them that it's hard *not* to also be reminded of that."

"I think I can understand that." Li nods. "It means a lot to you, then, coming here at all?"

"It does." Toreval's tail swishes sadly. "Thank you for giving me an excuse to come back. I've been... sort of cooped up in the city for a long time, now, doing my best to be strong for the rest of my family. I haven't been able to let myself truly process my own feelings, I think."

Li gives them a compassionate look for a few moments before he says anything. Having spent as much time around him as they now have, Toreval has begun to understand that even though he's one of the most straightforward humans they've ever met, he's still very careful to choose his words.

"Well," he says at last, smiling softly, "I'm glad you're getting to do that."

"So am I." Toreval returns the smile. They gesture through the somewhat narrow passageway in front of them. "And our destination is just on the other side here. I think you'll enjoy this."

"If there's anything I've learned about you, Celadon," Li quips, "it's that you have *excellent* taste in things to show me."

"Oh, do I?" Toreval giggles and offers him their lower pair of hands on a whim. "Here, let me show this one to you properly—assuming you trust me to lead you in with your eyes closed?"

Li chuckles. "Sure, why not?" He gently twines his own rather warm hands with their own and closes his eyes. "Just don't get lost in thought again, okay? I trust you to lead me, but I'd like to not get *actually* lost..."

"Cheeky human," Toreval teases. "Now, no peeking until I tell you, all right?"

"No peeking." Li repeats. "Lead the way."

Within a minute or two, Toreval has their human friend positioned so he's standing right in the middle of the grand crystal chamber, on the widest part of the shimmering transparent suspended walkway which leads from the passageway they were just in. They keep hold of his hands. They and Iralee did this with Johan, too—and considering that the sensation of looking down and only vaguely being able to see something supporting his feet was so jarring even to such an experienced caver, Toreval doesn't want to alarm Li too much.

"All right, Li, now before you open your eyes... I need you to trust me that you're just as safe right now as you were in the other passages. Can you do that?"

Li chuckles. "Sure. Why?"

"Take a look for yourself."

"Okay..."

Toreval grins as they see Li's pair of dark eyes slowly open, and then the twinned expressions of brief alarm and amazement cross his face as he looks down.

"What the—we're *floating*?" His hands squeeze Toreval's briefly.

"The walkway is. It's transparent so visitors can see the full extent of the crystals… Don't worry, the guardrails are there for a marker of where you can walk." Toreval is still grinning as they gesture with one of their upper hands to the myriad of purple, orange, and white crystals clinging to every surface of the chamber. "What do you think, Li?"

"I've never seen anything like it." Li's smile is almost as bright as the reflections of the lanterns suspended from the guardrails. "It's like standing in the center of a geode… *stars*, Celadon, this is incredible."

Toreval finds their tail waving happily. "I'm glad you like it. It's always been my favorite place in these caves. Maybe out of all the caves I've had a chance to visit, even."

"I can see why." Li marvels as he releases one of their hands and slowly turns to take in more of the scene all around him. "Some of these crystals are *huge*, too."

"The biggest ones are down there," Toreval tells him, pointing towards the chamber's distant floor, and the large shimmering spears of crystal jutting out from odd angles on the way down. "That's why the suspended walkway was designed this way—the caretakers of this place wanted people to be able to see them without physically disturbing anything."

"Or breaking an ankle or worse trying to walk through that forest of spikes, I'd imagine." Li nods appreciatively. "Those big ones have to be almost as tall as either of us… but I wouldn't want to try balancing on any of them."

"They're relatively sturdy, from what I'm told, but I don't think I'd want to test them either." Toreval chuckles.

"I like climbing and heights and all, but this is one place I'm content to just stand and enjoy the view."

"It's an amazing view, too." Li gives the hand he's still holding a small squeeze before releasing it, too, and cautiously walks over to one of the guardrails to get a better look at the nearby crystals. "Reminds me of being up in space, in a way."

"Oh?" Toreval takes a comfortable seat on the walkway with their legs crossed and looks up to him curiously.

"Yeah... That sort of 'being small in a good way' feeling from being weightless in an observation dome with nothing but the stars around you, if that means anything to you. Places like this remind a person how much of the universe there still is to see, and how much of an honor it is to get to live to see even as much of it as we do. There's all this *magnificence* around us, even in the smallest things... but it's harder to overlook when it's all around you like this." Li turns back to them with the same beaming look of serene fascination he wore when discussing orchids with Taldee. After a moment, he shakes his head with a self-deprecating chuckle in a way that makes the long hanging portion of his high looped ponytail swish softly. "Forgive me, Celadon, if that's too far afield... I was raised around Artisans; sometimes I forget myself."

"I know exactly what you mean, though, Li." Toreval can't help smiling at him. They've not met many humans who so intuitively speak to their own feelings on the wonders the reality they live in has to offer. More than that, his voice bears a bright warmth when he talks like this that they can't help but feel drawn towards. "Don't expect me to judge you for saying things like that—I *am* Florivan, remember?" They make a pointed, teasing gesture with their tail for emphasis.

"True." Li laughs and comes to sit beside them, taking out his water bottle once more. "You probably understand all of that better than I do."

"I think we understand in our own ways." Toreval shrugs, looking up to the sparkling shards of the chandelier-like crystal formations above them. "My people chose yours for our friends because we were *compatibly* different, after all... our perceptions compliment each other."

"Well, then." Li raises his water bottle to them as if making a toast. "Here's to friendship and the wonders around us."

"Indeed." Toreval toasts him with their own water bottle before taking a sip. The thought flits through their mind that they're very fortunate to have this particular human be the one they needed to get to know for the Council's sake. Even if their friendship with Li can only ever be temporary, they couldn't ask for a more pleasant companion for an afternoon's adventure.

Part 2: The River Festival

T HE RIVER FESTIVAL HAS ALWAYS BEEN ONE OF Toreval's favorite events of the year. It's held in the final weeks of the jungle's dryer season, which usually means that the weather is in a mood to cooperate and not send up sudden thunderstorms to spoil everyone's fun.

Today, as befits the opening day of the Festival, the sky is clear and the air is pleasantly warm without being overbearingly hot even by Florivan standards. All of the Elders who live in City-on-the-River have gathered their households around the banks of the River in the various terraces and gardens for a week-long celebration full of picnics, dancing, and storytelling. Quite a few more of the Elders from the Sanctuary's other cities are in attendance than usual as well, thanks to the call that has gone out for the upcoming Full Session of the Council. Toreval is always amazed at the number of their people who attend the Festival, but this year is particularly notable for just how many of them have gathered. The majority of their people's two hundred thousand or so adults and Elders still live at Procyon, and Toreval wouldn't be surprised if at least a tenth of that are in the City this week.

Their species has quite a meager population, compared to their human friends, but in truth it's finally started to grow again now that the devastating waves of the so-called 'Periodic Jungle Plague' are a thing of the past. Toreval themself was so small of a kitten during the last of those that their eyes weren't even open yet, but the disease touched their life even if they don't remember it. The Jungle Plague had taken their littermates and a majority of their parent's extended family, by the time it ended—a story which is far from uncommon among their people. Toreval can only hope that theirs will be the last generation of Florivans to ever have to grow up in the wake of such a trauma.

Today, though, is a celebration of *life* and the triumph of their people over their long history of adversity and tragic losses. The river flows down from its headwaters in the high mountains of the deeper jungle, cascading down the tall waterfalls and then meandering through the city and down all the way to the far-distant sea. Toreval's people are alive, and they are *together*. The great extended family of all Florivans now living is represented here, and it is a perfect day for a family picnic by the water.

Up on the floating translucent stage that has been suspended between the two bridges which cross the river near the base of the waterfall, Elder Kyanite and the other Star-keepers are presenting the first of the stories from the

River Cycle: The Exploration Up The Long River. Toreval watches with delight from their seat beside the Eldest in the viewing pavilion that's been erected on the bridge further from the waterfall as the dear survivor-smallest of their own first litter takes on the lyrically pantomimed role of the river's first explorer while Elder Kyanite recites the story.

"Your Ilmi's a natural for the part," the Eldest whispers to Toreval, nudging them lightly with their lower elbow.

"They really are," Toreval agrees, still watching. "They wouldn't let me come to watch more than two or three of the practices, but it's *amazing* seeing it all put together..."

"Shh!" little Myrval admonishes softly with a twitch of their ears from where they're sitting at Toreval and the Eldest's feet between Marbree and Taldee. "This is the best part."

Toreval and the Eldest exchange amused glances with their third eyes while keeping the rest of their attention on the performance. The kitten's right, though; the story has nearly reached its climax, with Ilmi as the first explorer being lifted up into the air by several of the accompanying dancers to represent the legendary fall their direct ancestor took from the peak of the waterfall.

Ilmi never falters once in their performance, even though it requires them to balance one of the larger star-keeping spheres in their upper hands while making all of the broad leaps and dance-like gestures necessary to convey their part—a testament to the months of careful practice and rehearsals they've undertaken. This is a big day for Ilmi: it's the first time since they returned from their apprenticeship and declared their intention for the Star-

Keeper's path that they've been assigned such a central part in one of the Festival stories. Toreval couldn't be prouder of their kitten.

They only wish that Inayan and Iralee were here to see their littermate doing such a good job. Iralee in particular had always shared Ilmi's love of the old stories and the performance tradition, although they never sought to make that their path in life the way Ilmi has; the stars called to them too loudly.

Toreval has fond memories of being the sole member of the audience as their three eldest kittens put on miniature performances of the different story cycles in their home's sitting room, though. Inayan always went along with it for the sake of their littermates and a chance to dress up in borrowed bits of cloth from Toreval's closet, while little Ilmi was always the narrator and Iralee did the more acrobatic parts of the dancing. Toreval had recorded a few of the performances to send to their parent and the Eldest, too—they'd forgotten about that, until now, but with a bittersweet nostalgia they know now that they'll have to find those recordings in their files to treat Ilmi and Taldee to later this evening. Taldee was too young to remember the game at the time, after all.

The story reaches its end, with Ilmi standing in the center of the stage with the star-keeping orb held high above their head while the other Star-Keepers wave the long piece of translucent blue silk representing the River along the stage and bring it to be draped around Ilmi's feet as if forming a magnificent splash. The projected lights swirl around them on the mists from the waterfall to enhance the illusion. Elder Kyanite pronounces the end of the story with a flourish.

Toreval stands to applaud the performers, as do the Eldest and the kittens sitting with the two of them. The rest of the gathered audience follows suit, cheering for a magnificent opening to the week's festivities.

"Your big sib is *awesome*!" Toreval hears Marbree telling Taldee.

"They are!" Taldee agrees. "Ilmi took me to one of their practices and showed me how they do the thing where it looks like they're flying—that's the best part!"

Toreval stifles a giggle. It's nice to see that the kittens enjoyed the performance too. They settle a hand on Taldee's head to signal them to settle down as the crowd's attention turns towards their place on the viewing platform.

"Eldest, Youngest," calls Elder Kyanite from the narrator's perch above the stage, now that the applause is quieting enough that their enhanced voice can be heard again and they can recite the final part of the Festival opening ceremony. "We present these tales from our people's past to you and to all who are gathered here, the gift of our ancestors as is this Sanctuary they built for us all. We tell their stories that they may live on, that our kittens and all who come after us may remember who we are as a people and be guided by their example, their hope, and their courage."

"We gladly accept this gift, Elder Kyanite," the Eldest intones, using their most formal voice, "on behalf of all who are gathered here." They pause, making a sweeping gesture to the banks of the river with each of their upper hands. The lower two remain resting lightly on their cane.

"As the guardian of our people's past and traditions, I thank you and all your fellow Star-Keepers for your continued efforts."

"And as the guardian of our people's future," says Toreval, doing their best to match the Eldest's tone as they recite their own portion of the ritual, "I promise you that the stories you tell will be carried forward as our people continue to make our way in this world."

Elder Kyanite bows in the direction of the viewing platform with a dramatic flourish that makes the saffron shades of their robes seem to sparkle. Ilmi and the other Star-Keepers on the stage do the same.

"With that," says the Eldest, brighter-toned now, "we declare this Festival of the River officially begun!"

Another cheer goes up from the gathered crowd. The Eldest sits back down with a genial smile as the projected image of them and Toreval disappears from the mists of the waterfall.

As the Star-Keepers begin to leave the stage and prepare for their next, less elaborate performance, Toreval feels a light tug on the edge of their robes. They turn their eyes downwards to see Taldee beaming up at them, their tail swishing excitedly.

"Does this mean Ilmi can come play in the water with us now, Nida?"

"I think they may be busy for the rest of the day, dear," says Toreval, their third eye turning back to the stage to seek out Ilmi. They spot their kitten in the middle of all of the older Star-Keepers, happily accepting congratulatory hugs from their mentors. "But perhaps they'll have some time this evening to come swim with you."

Taldee's ears droop in disappointment.

"In the meantime, Taldee," the Eldest interjects with a conspiratorial glance between their own two youngest kittens and Toreval, "perhaps you could go down to the shallow water with Marbree and Myrval? I'm sure the three of you can find one of your adult cousins there who's free to swim with you now, since your Nida and I are stuck being 'official' today."

Taldee immediately perks up, their tail swishing as they tug on Toreval's robe again. "Can we, Nida?"

"Of course," says Toreval, gathering their kitten up into a hug. "Just stay close to Marbree and Myrval, okay? We'll come down to watch you swim in a bit."

"Come on, then!" Marbree takes both the younger kitten and their littermate by the hand. "Let's go find someone to play with!"

With that, the three of them scamper off the viewing platform and disappear into the colorful bustle of the awnings set up along the riverbank.

Toreval looks to the Eldest with a teasing smile. "How long do you think it'll take those three to find some mischief to get into?"

The Eldest laughs. "Considering that Marbree is just like I was as a kitten and Taldee seems to have even *more* of your trouble-maker streak than any of your first litter inherited... half an hour at the most."

"That long?" Toreval raises all three eyebrows.

"Well, Myrval is with them, and they're just as much a calming influence as your Ilmi is—most of the time." The Eldest twitches their ears with amusement. "Speaking of whom, shall we go congratulate our youngest Star-Keeper on their good work, since we only have to look official for the rest of the day and aren't stuck sitting up here like part of the decorations?"

Toreval offers the Eldest their lower arm. "I'd be delighted."

It doesn't take long for the two of them to make their way down to the preparation tent that's been set up near the stage. The tent is bustling with activity as different props and costumes are being sorted out for the group of dancers who will be performing next. Ilmi is busy packing the large crystal star-keeping sphere back into its padded carrying case when Toreval and the Eldest enter.

"Ilmi," says Toreval, approaching their kitten with all four arms outstretched, "you were *magnificent*."

Ilmi happily accepts the hug, even lightly wrapping their tail around Toreval for a moment for good measure. "Thank you, Nida. I'm glad you enjoyed the performance."

"I did." Toreval lightly ruffles Ilmi's ears, being careful not to jostle out any of the strings of beads and ribbons that are woven into their hair. "I'm so proud of you, kitten—and I know your littermates would be too."

Ilmi lets out a small, bittersweet sigh. "You think so?"

Toreval hugs them closer. "I know so."

After a long moment of silence, when Toreval finally lets go of their kitten, the Eldest speaks up. "I'd like to congratulate you too, dear. You take on the lyric role with more spirit than anyone I've seen in a long time. You certainly do a better job at it than *I* ever did when I was your age, for that matter."

"Thank you, Eldest." Ilmi beams and accepts a congratulatory hug from them too. "I've been nervous about it all week..."

"Understandable," says the Eldest, smiling, "but you're doing well."

"Thank you." Ilmi dips their head respectfully, then looks between Toreval and the Eldest with open curiosity. "Where's Taldee? I thought they'd be with you."

"We let them and Marbree and Myrval go down to the shallow water to play—assuming they can find an adult to swim with." Toreval chuckles. "Although they're still holding out hope that you'll be free this evening."

"Ah." Ilmi nods lightly. "Well, those three will be fine for the day, then—"

"—Jade dear," Elder Kyanite calls from the stage, "Can you come help me with these banners?"

"Just a minute!" Ilmi calls back. They look up to Toreval with a pointedly teasing look. "You'll *try* not to get into any mischief today, won't you, Nida?"

Toreval pats their kitten on the head and gives them a matching look. "Now, *really*, how am I supposed to cause chaos when you make me promise things like that?"

The Eldest laughs. "Don't worry, dear, I'll keep an eye on them. We're both supposed to be on our best behavior today, you know."

Ilmi looks between the two Elders in front of them, then shakes their head. "Well, Eldest, I can't ask for more than that... save me a seat at dinner?"

"Of course." Toreval stifles a giggle. "Monica promised she'd bring a whole basket of those buns you like, too."

"Now that's worth looking forward to." Ilmi's eyes light up. "I'll see you then!" With a jingling swish of their tail, they turn and scamper off onto the translucent polyglass of the stage to see to whatever it is that Elder Kyanite needed their help sorting out.

Toreval turns to the Eldest. "How in the stars did I end up with a kitten who worries about *me* getting into trouble more than they do their little sibling?"

The Eldest chuckles, giving Toreval a knowing look. "Well, dear, they *were* always a bit more cautious than the rest of your kittens... and you can't really fault them for being aware of your reputation."

Toreval sighs, shaking their head lightly as they and the Eldest leave the preparation tent to meander along the riverbank. "Considering that they've spent their whole life hearing everyone tell the most embarrassingly exaggerated stories, I probably shouldn't be surprised."

"Jade reminds me so much of my Rain," the Eldest begins, using their respective kittens' public names now that they're no longer talking in private amongst close family. "They were like that too—but then, back when Rain and their littermates were Jade's age, *I* was the Council's troublesome Youngest..."

Toreval knows the faraway nostalgic tone in the Eldest's voice all too well. It's the same one that they find themself taking on whenever their thoughts turn to Iralee and Inayan.

Rain was one of the Eldest's first kittens—a survivor-smallest, like Ilmi—and well-known by many of their people as a brilliant healer. Rain was also among the final victims of the last wave of the Jungle Plague, succumbing to the illness themself mere months after saving Toreval's own newly-begun life. It was in Rain's honor, too, that Toreval was named once their eyes opened. They've always been proud of sharing their private name with someone who gave everything to help their people.

Toreval smiles gently. "I've always wished I could have remembered them."

"They'd have adored you and your kittens, dear, I'm sure." The Eldest sighs and pats Toreval's arm where their hand is already resting on it. After a moment, they return to their more accustomed cheerfulness. "And speaking of our kittens... shall we go see who they've gotten into the water?"

"Yes, Eldest." Toreval chuckles. "Now, if we can just find a way to wind up in the water *ourselves...*"

The Eldest shakes their head, although their ears are twitching with amusement. "Now, now, dear, we're being well-behaved today, remember? *Tomorrow* we can fall in the water and pretend we didn't mean to all we like."

Toreval tries to be solemn in their responding nod, but they only barely manage not to giggle. "Of course, Eldest."

WHEN TOREVAL AND THE ELDEST FINALLY MAKE their way down to the shallower area of the riverbed that the current nets and floating barriers have been set up around so the kittens around Taldee's age can play and swim safely without being swept away, it's been almost three hours since they left Ilmi at the Story-Keepers' preparation tent. The two of them are far too distinct in their robes not to be stopped by every other family whose bright-colored pavilion they pass and be engaged in pleasant conversation over tea, light snacks, and cooling fruit juices.

They find little Myrval first, who is *not* out splashing in the water, but sitting contentedly on the bottommost dry step of the wide staircase leading down to the river with their feet dangling over the edge into the gentle current. Sitting beside Myrval with her trouser-legs rolled up into shorts and her feet similarly dangling in the water is none other than Admiral Marvin. On the other side of the Admiral is a small, somewhat-tidy pile of shoes, clothing, and towels. Myrval's white tunic and trousers are among the pile, as they've changed into a pair of swimming shorts and have one of the towels loosely draped over their otherwise-bare shoulders. They and the Admiral seem to be engaged in a genial conversation about the merits of various Earth waterfowl as Toreval and the Eldest approach.

"—And I tell you, River, that goose *never* let me walk through grandmother's garden to collect up the eggs without making a big hissy fuss after that," says the Admiral, shaking her head.

Myrval looks up to her with wide eyes and a curious swish of the tip of their tail. "Are *all* domesticated geese so intimidating?"

The Admiral chuckles. "Let's just say some of them are more touchy than others, but most of them have those little moments now and again... and that half the reason I went into space as a girl was to get away from them."

Myrval seems to consider this for a moment, then gives the Admiral a cheerful shrug. "I'd still like to meet one someday!"

"Perhaps, River," interjects the Eldest, now that they and Toreval are nearly standing behind the kitten and the Admiral, "when *Deinocheirus* next makes port at one of the human agricultural planets, you and Ocean can arrange to go down and visit some of these birds."

Myrval looks up with a hopeful sparkle in all three of their eyes. "Do you think so, Nida? That would be *stellar—*

maybe I could find a way to make friends with a goose so it wouldn't want to hiss and chase me…"

The Eldest stifles a giggle. "You'll have to send me pictures when you do, dear." They turn to the Admiral with a genial nod. "Good afternoon, Admiral Marvin; I see my kittens are doing a good job at extending our hospitality to you."

"Good afternoon, Eldest, Youngest." The Admiral makes a move to stand, but a gesture from the Eldest stops her. She smiles and settles back into her seat beside Myrval. "And yes, they're being excellent hosts. River here has been letting me reminisce about home a bit—not often I get to do that, anymore."

"She grew up on *Earth*," says Myrval with no small amount of excitement, "at a real human-style farmstead with *ducks* and *chickens* and things."

The Eldest smiles and reaches down to ruffle their kitten's ears briefly. "And geese, from what I overheard. I'm glad the two of you have found something to talk about." They slip off their sandals discretely and take a seat next to Myrval, carefully tucking the longer portions of the white silks of their robes up so they won't get wet as they, too, dangle their feet into the water. This done, the Eldest lets out a contented sigh and pats the empty spot beside them, looking up to Toreval with their third eye.

Toreval happily accepts the invitation, similarly setting their sandals aside and tucking up the amber layers of their own robes. The water is just the right amount of pleasantly cool to be refreshing against their skin. It's nice to be able to sit down properly for a moment, too, considering all of the standing and walking they've been doing today in order to be appropriately social with all of the people that have called to them and the Eldest.

"Now," says the Eldest, looking to little Myrval with a curious tilt of their head. "Where might Ocean and your cousin Lapis be?"

Myrval makes a small gesture out towards the water. "Not far, Nida. They're both out swimming."

"You didn't want to go with them?" asks the Eldest, setting one of their upper arms over the top of the towel around the adolescent's shoulders.

"Oh, I will later... but the water was *cold*." Myrval contentedly settles into their parent's side. Like most survivor-smallest kittens, they're still of a more delicate constitution than others their age; Ilmi was much the same way, when they were younger, being far more cautious and aware of their own tendency to get chilled. "Besides, someone needed to keep Admiral Marvin company."

"Who did the three of you find to swim with, in the end?" Toreval asks, turning their attention out towards the water to look for Taldee and Marbree amongst the group of similarly-aged kittens who are splashing about in the shallows with their respective older siblings or entiles.

"They're borrowing my assistant for the afternoon," the Admiral answers with a chuckle, pointing in the appropriate direction.

When Toreval looks, they're amused and slightly surprised to see both their youngest and Marbree splashing with Li in the deeper part of the enclosed swimming area. The three of them look to be having a grand time of it, too. The water comes up to about the level of Li's mid-chest when he stands up, while both kittens seem to be lightly treading water beside him. While he's still wearing his green short-sleeved undershirt, the young human seems to have retrieved and changed into a pair of swimming shorts just as Myrval and the other kittens have.

"Hsu Li is a very good swimmer," adds Myrval, appreciatively. "Taldee introduced us to him, and he agreed to be our adult to swim with for the rest of the Festival since the two of you and Jade have to be busy."

"That's very kind of him," Toreval says, watching Li pick Taldee up out of the water and toss them up so they can make a big splash as they fall back into it. They shake their head. Leave it to Taldee to seek out *Li* to play with instead of any of the many adults of their own species that they know.

"I'm grateful the three of them came up and asked him," says the Admiral. "I'd thought this 'local guide' friend he's mentioned would be around today so I could meet them, but from what Ensign Hsu has said, they're busy with Festival matters—and while I *am* enjoying the event myself, it's good to see him being induced to relax and not think he needs to constantly hover around me."

Toreval barely manages to maintain their composure when the Admiral mentions them unknowingly. They're glad to know, though, that she doesn't seem to have any awareness of just who Li's Florivan friend *is*.

"They *do* look like they're all having fun," says the Eldest, giving Toreval a subtle nudge with the fluffy tip of their tail.

"They do at that," Toreval agrees. They chuckle as they turn their eyes back out to the water.

Li boosts Marbree up into the air this time, who manages to *thoroughly* soak him with their splash as they land back into the water. From the looks of it, a number of the other kittens out swimming have noticed the young human playing with Taldee and Marbree and are beginning to circle up around him to ask to join the game as well.

"We've been taking pictures for your family albums, Nida," Myrval informs the Eldest, grinning. "I'll show you tonight!"

"Why, thank you, River." The Eldest flashes a similar grin. "I was just about to ask if you had—we'll have to pick some of those to send to your older siblings later."

"Do you want copies too, Celadon?" Myrval asks, looking over to Toreval.

"Of course—"

"—Hi, Nida! Hi, Celadon!" Just as Toreval is beginning to speak, Marbree splashes over to where the four of them are sitting. "River!" they call, waving excitedly, "come on! We've made up a new game and you *have* to come play it with us!" Marbree takes hold of their littermate's hands with an expectant, splashy swish of their tail.

"Do I?" asks Myrval, narrowing their eyes slightly at Marbree.

"Yes!" Marbree giggles. Their tail makes droplets of water spray all over the place with its excited swishing. "Didn't you see Hsu Li tossing us up in the air? It's great fun—and you're *smaller* than either of us, so we think you'll be able to fly *higher* and make a better splash!"

"Well..." little Myrval looks up at their parent now.

"Go on, dear," says the Eldest, making an encouraging gesture with their hands. "I'll stay here for a few minutes more to watch you."

This, in the end, is all the encouragement Myrval needs to let their littermate pull them into the water. The two adolescents splash their way over to where Li and Taldee are waiting.

True to form, the Eldest has their pocket-com out to take pictures almost as soon as the kittens leave them. "I'll send copies of all of these to you, dear," they say, their third eye briefly glancing Toreval's direction.

"Thank you, Eldest," Toreval says, stifling a giggle.

The Eldest makes a point of taking *lots* of pictures of all of the kittens in their life—they have entire bookcases in their home dedicated to their collection of physical picture-albums, even. Toreval has a few such albums themself too, now, in addition to the digital files they keep. Three of their albums were gifts from the Eldest: one documenting their kittenhood and extended family, and two more dedicated to their own kittens.

According to the Eldest, the practice of keeping all of the pictures of their family isn't just pleasing because it helps them to remember all of the good times they've had with the people they care about most; it's a good way to introduce the kittens to the members of their family that they might not know otherwise. With all of the losses the older Florivan has experienced over the years and the number of their living kittens who are out among the stars, it's more common than not that their younger litters will never meet their siblings and entiles in person.

Toreval had always thought it was a sweet sort of a pastime, but it wasn't until images were all they had left of Inayan and Iralee that they truly understood the reasoning behind it. Now, even though they weren't able to bring themself to look through their albums for months after the news reached them, they cherish every memory held in those pages.

Their musing on the subject is brief, though, and quickly overshadowed by the spectacle of Li tossing little Myrval up into the air as high as he can and the subsequent splash the kitten makes upon landing back in the water with all their limbs drawn inwards. The water spray goes far enough to shower all of the other kittens who've come closer to watch, as well as several of the adults who are out there swimming with them.

Squeals of delight echo all around the roped-off area of the river. The Eldest, Toreval, and even Admiral Marvin add their voices to the cacophony of applause for good measure.

"Now *that*," says the Eldest, showing the Admiral and Toreval the little video clip they've filmed alongside the pictures they were taking, "is worth sending to Sky and Stream!"

Toreval can't help giggling. "They'll both be jealous, that's for sure. It does look like fun, doesn't it?"

"It does," says the Eldest, slipping the pocket-com back into the folds of their robes. They give Toreval a teasing glance. "If we weren't having to be official today, I'd say you should go out there and see if the Ensign will toss *you* too..."

"Eldest!" Toreval laughs, covering their face dramatically with both upper hands for a moment. "And people say *I'm* the Council's troublemaker…"

"Oh, I don't know, Youngest," Admiral Marvin quips, "I get the feeling you'd make a very nice splash."

Toreval looks over to the human with an incredulous twitch of their ears. "Possibly, yes—and then it'd be months before I'd hear the end of it, if ever. I've had *six* people tease me about falling in by accident as it is today."

"You fell in?" The human tilts her head curiously.

"Not *today*."

"They fall in every year, sooner or later," says the Eldest, clearly making a show of using their formal voice. "Whether it's *always* an accident when they do is anyone's guess."

The Admiral chuckles. "With a day like this, I can see how one might want to 'accidentally' fall into the water…"

Toreval gives the Eldest their best wide-eyed why-must-you-embarrass-me-in-front-of-this-human sort of look, then sighs and pointedly turns their attention back towards their youngest kitten and Li. They slip their own pocket-com out to take some pictures while Li is tossing Taldee into the water again.

They can't help smiling, seeing how happy Taldee is playing with Li and all of the other kittens. Their youngest has gone through a bit of a quiet phase over the last few months, between their two best friends leaving to start their apprenticeships and the news of losing two of their older siblings. It's nice to see Taldee acting like the little 'ball of lightning' they've always been once more, and Toreval's sure it's in no small part due to their newfound friendship with Li. The young human seems to bring out the joy in the kittens almost instinctively.

They *do* have a strong impulse themself to get into the water and play with their youngest and their human friend, but Toreval knows they should probably make sure that they're not still sitting here when Li eventually tires of playing water games with the crowd of excited kittens who are now surrounding him. It wouldn't do, after all, to have him potentially recognize them out of their disguise—and since Taldee doesn't fully understand that Toreval *has* been in disguise this whole time, they would probably give it all away too. Toreval isn't ready for him to know who they really are, not yet.

They watch for a few more minutes while the Eldest and the Admiral make small talk about the River and the upcoming events of the Festival, and then finally sigh and stand to collect their shoes. "I hate to have to leave," says Toreval, bowing to the Eldest, "but I did promise Elder Caeruleus I'd speak to them today... do you mind terribly if I go do that now while I have a few minutes free?"

"Not at all, dear," says the Eldest, giving them a knowingly genial smile. "I'm content to stay here for a while. I'll watch over Lapis for you—and don't worry, I'll save some of my plum scones for you and Ilmi to have this evening if I don't see you at teatime."

Toreval nods, unable to hide their grin. "Thank you, Eldest. Good day, Admiral Marvin."

With that, albeit reluctantly, Toreval walks up the stairs to the riverbank pathway and into the crowd. Today, they do have other things that they need to do—not the least of which *is* discussing matters with Elder Caeruleus—

but tomorrow? Tomorrow will be a good day to fall into
the water with their kittens.

A few days after the River Festival ends, Toreval comes home from a pleasant day of hiking through one of the City Arboretum's more winding nature trails with Li to find both of their kittens upset. Their keen catlike ears pick up the unaccustomed sounds of heated arguing between Ilmi and Taldee before they even open the door, although they can't make out precisely what the words are.

Needless to say, Toreval is concerned when they walk in.

"Kittens?" Toreval calls, doing their best to keep their voice calm and cheerful as they close the door behind them. "I'm home—is everything all right?"

"Nida!" Immediately, Taldee rushes to them from the sitting room and wraps all four arms around Toreval's legs, burying their lightly damp face in the folds of Toreval's soft grey tunic. They say something, but it's muffled by all the fabric.

Toreval sets a gentle hand on their youngest kitten's head and begins lightly stroking their hair. "It's all right, Taldee, I'm here. Now, what happened?"

Once again, what little reply Taldee gives is mumbled into the folds of Toreval's tunic and impossible to understand as words. Their tail wraps around Toreval, too.

Ilmi appears now, standing in the arched doorway between the entry hall and the sitting room. They look just as thoroughly upset as Taldee, although in a way that has them crossing all four arms and staring Toreval down.

"Ilmi?" Toreval asks gently, still petting Taldee's hair and ears to settle them down so they'll be willing to speak, "Do you think you can explain this?"

"Oh, I'm sure *you'll* have more of the explanation than I do, Nida," Ilmi says dryly, although with more hurt coloring their tone than sarcasm. "Because all I know for certain is that I went to pick them up from Entile Indigo's for our lesson this evening—because they were *late* meeting me again—and I found them just—" Ilmi wrinkles their nose in disdain. "—Just *sitting there* with that suspicious human Admiral who's visiting, talking up a storm like the two of them are fast friends and she's *not* to blame for—"

"—But she's *nice!*" Taldee interrupts, looking up to Toreval now with moist eyes as their words spill out all at once. "I don't understand why I'm in trouble, Nida, but Ilmi's mad at me and I was just talking to her about starships and how I want to be a Ranger someday like Iralee and Inayan, and—and Ilmi says I'm not supposed to play with her, but humans are our *friends* and Admiral Marvin is *your* friend too, like Hsu Li is, isn't she? So why—"

"—You *knew*?" Ilmi's tone and expression as they turn their eyes to Toreval are a mixture of horrified shock and *hurt*. "Nida, how could you let them—"

"*Kittens*," says Toreval, in their gentlest but firmest parental voice, "settle down."

In the tense silence that follows, they sigh lightly and scoop Taldee up into their arms, grateful that their youngest is still small enough to easily be picked up and carried. With Taldee's face buried against their shoulder now, they calmly walk over and set their free upper hand on Ilmi's shoulder.

"I've never seen the two of you at odds with each other like this before... and I suppose it's my fault that you are. Now, will you both take a moment to breathe while I sort this out?"

Ilmi sighs, their tail twitching with a pointed agitation that makes the little bangles on it jingle. "Yes, Nida."

"Yes, Nida," Taldee echoes, although their whisper is muffled by the cloth of Toreval's tunic.

"Good." Toreval guides Ilmi into the sitting room and motions for them to take a seat on the plush green couch. They continue holding Taldee close while they settle themself into a comfortable position beside Ilmi.

Both kittens are silent in a brooding, agitated sort of way. The bangles on Ilmi's tail jingle softly every time that agitation makes it twitch.

"Now," Toreval says, settling their free upper arm around Ilmi's shoulders, "am I to understand that the center of this disagreement is that Taldee's been allowed to spend time with our human visitors, and I'd neglected to tell you that I approved of that?"

Ilmi crosses both pairs of arms over their chest and looks away. Their voice still sounds pained, even if they seem to be doing their best to conceal that. "...Yes, Nida, that's the short version of it."

"I'd like to apologize to you for that, Ilmi." Toreval gives Ilmi's shoulder a gentle squeeze. "As Taldee's mentor, I should have explained it to you... and as their older sibling, I should have understood that you'd be concerned about them interacting with someone who makes you uncomfortable."

Ilmi turns their third eye back towards Toreval and nods silently that they accept the apology. They subtly relax, although their arms are still crossed and their tail is still twitching at its fluffy silver tip.

"But Admiral Marvin is nice," Taldee interjects, as little more than a confused whisper, "and so is Hsu Li... and I like talking to them..."

"I know, dear." Toreval lightly begins to stroke the kitten's hair. "And I'm sorry that my oversight has led to upsetting you. Ilmi has their reasons for being cautious around her, though, and we need to respect that."

Taldee lets out a disappointed little sigh and looks over to Ilmi with all three eyes wide and pleading. "You'd like her, though, Ilmi, if you got to know her—"

"—I don't intend to *ever* talk to that human, much less 'get to know her.'" Ilmi cuts them off with a barb in their tone that's clearly meant for Toreval rather than their little sibling. "And I *don't* like her having the chance to manipulate you."

Taldee looks back up to Toreval with hurt in their eyes now and a sad droop to their ears. "But she's *your* friend, isn't she, Nida? Like Hsu Li is?"

"I'm acquainted with her because of her business with the Council." Toreval finds themself unable to hold back a sigh. "And that's the same reason I've been spending time with her assistant, in the end."

Taldee gives them a confused and disappointed expression. "But he's your *friend*."

Toreval hesitates. How can they deny it? "He is, yes, but once the Admiral's business here is done, he'll be leaving with her. And as far as I understand, Ilmi isn't as uncomfortable with him?" They look over to their older kitten with a questioning twitch of their ears.

"The Ensign works for *her*," Ilmi says, with a darker barb in their tone, but then they relent a bit. "And I'm not interested in being friends with him either, but if spending time with him is part of your work, Nida, I can understand that."

"Thank you." Toreval feels a small flash of relief, although they don't have time to think about why. "Now, I'd like to suggest a solution to all of this, if the two of you are willing?"

Both kittens nod silently.

"Good. Taldee? You want to know more about the humans who visit us in preparation for starting your apprenticeship in a few years, yes?"

"Yes, Nida." Taldee gives their older sibling a pointed glare with their third eye, keeping the lower two hopeful and looking up at Toreval. "*I* like humans, even if Ilmi doesn't."

"I know you do, dear," says Toreval, doing their best to not sound amused at that. "And Ilmi? You'd like to know who Taldee is talking to and what they're being told?"

"...Yes, Nida," Ilmi tells them reluctantly, "at the *very least* I'd like to be aware of that, if you're set on allowing them to spend time around people like the ones you have to work with."

"Okay, then." Toreval gives their older kitten's shoulder a reassuring squeeze. "What I'd like to suggest is that we make this part of Taldee's education. They'll interview the different humans who live in the city or are here visiting, and then submit reports on each one to you, Ilmi, as part of their lessons from now on. That way, you'll have an idea of who they're interacting with, and they'll be learning more about our people's friends and what to expect when they go out into the stars as an apprentice when the time comes. Does that sound acceptable to both of you?"

"Yes, Nida!" Taldee's ears perk up. "That would be *neat*!"

"I... suppose I could be okay with that," says Ilmi with a sigh. "At least then they'll be making an effort to be around humans *other* than the Admiral."

"Good, I thought so." Toreval pulls both of their kittens in close for a few moments. "Now," they say, as they let go of the hug, "would the two of you please apologize to each other?"

Taldee nods and shifts over into their older sibling's lap to give them a proper hug. "I'm sorry I was late for lessons and didn't tell you who I was playing with, Ilmi," they say. "I didn't know you were scared of her."

"I'm not *afraid* of her, Taldee. I just... don't like her very much." Ilmi flashes their eyes towards Toreval pointedly over the top of Taldee's head. Their tone softens as they look back down into their little sibling's expectant face. "And I'm sorry I reacted the way I did and upset you."

The two kittens share a snuggle of forgiveness. Toreval can't help being grateful that they were able to resolve the matter without further upsetting either of them. It's not often that they've had to use their "parent voice" and interfere in disagreements between their kittens. They only wish they'd been able to prevent this one from happening in the first place.

"Is it okay if I go to a sleepover with Marbree and Myrval tonight?" Taldee asks their sibling at last, sounding like their usual chipper self again. "They'd asked if I'd come earlier, but I didn't get a chance to ask *you* yet because you were mad at me."

"I'm not mad at *you*, Taldee," Ilmi tells them, their third eye glancing to Toreval. "I'm okay with it if Nida is. I don't think I'm in the right frame of mind for lessons anymore this evening anyway."

"Nida?" Taldee looks to Toreval with eager, hopeful eyes.

"Of course you can go, dear," says Toreval, reaching over to ruffle both kittens' ears before they stand up and stretch out their limbs. "I'll take you down to meet them as soon as I get changed back into my robes—It'll give me and Ilmi some time alone, too, and I think there's some things we need to talk about."

"There are at that," says Ilmi with one more jingling twitch of their tail.

★

It's dusk when Toreval walks to the Eldest's home with Taldee. Their youngest kitten is uncharacteristically silent for the first half of the walk, before they finally look up and tug on one of the sleeves of Toreval's robe to catch their attention.

"Nida?"

"Yes, Taldee?" Toreval turns their lower two eyes down to look at their kitten.

"Why doesn't Ilmi like humans?"

"I don't think it's *all* humans they distrust, really, dear," Toreval replies with a sigh. "But the Admiral makes them uncomfortable... and any other humans who work for the Fleet or the Rangers do as well, I suspect."

"I don't understand. The Admiral and Hsu Li are so *nice*, and all of the Rangers who come here are too... like Johan and Rick were."

"I know, Taldee." Toreval sighs. They'd liked Iralee and Inayan's counterparts just as much as Taldee had. "But for Ilmi..." It takes a moment to find the right words to explain it to their youngest kitten. "Well. Do you remember how *long* it took them to get to be friends with Johan and Rick, and why it was hard for them?"

Taldee nods. "Because they were sad that Iralee and Inayan weren't going to live with us anymore?"

"Right." That's a drastic simplification, of course, but it's close enough. "Ilmi didn't want to like Johan and Rick, but they learned to in the end because *Iralee and Inayan* liked the two of them so much—and Johan and Rick made a very determined effort to be friends with Ilmi and prove that they'd be good counterparts for their littermates, even when Ilmi wasn't particularly friendly towards them."

"I miss them," Taldee whispers.

Toreval scoops their kitten up to carry them for the rest of the walk. "I do to, dear, and so does Ilmi. *That's* why they're so cautious about humans now, and why they don't like Admiral Marvin."

"I don't understand."

"Well," says Toreval, gently, "Iralee and Inayan had been working with the Admiral... and Ilmi is still grieving just like we are, but their way of doing that is partly to find someone to blame for what happened who they can direct all of the anger and pain they're feeling towards."

Taldee is silent for a moment. "Ilmi thinks it's Admiral Marvin's fault that they're gone?"

"Not just hers," Toreval admits with a sigh, "but yes."

"*Oh*. No wonder they were upset." Taldee's ears droop, and then they look back to Toreval with a curious tilt of their head. "But *you* don't think that, do you, Nida?"

"No, dear. I... I think she's done the best she could under the circumstances." Toreval hesitates. "I suppose the best way to put it is that I've decided to forgive her for her part in what happened, because my way of working through the grief is to try and do what Iralee and Inayan would have wanted me to. They both thought Admiral Marvin was worthy of their trust, and now that I've finally met her, I've decided to respect that."

"Okay." Taldee nods. They grow quiet again, but in a contented way. "Can I still interview her and Hsu Li for my lessons?"

"Yes, Taldee, of course. Just make sure you interview some other humans too, for Ilmi's sake."

Taldee giggles. "I'll interview Auntie Monica first! If I bring home the buns Ilmi likes, maybe they'll decide to like letting me interview people."

"Now, there's an idea!" Toreval chuckles. "Save a bun for me, will you?"

"I will!"

Not long after dropping Taldee off at the Eldest's home, Toreval is once again sitting on the couch with Ilmi. Their eldest kitten, it seems, spent the entire time they were gone in much the same spot as Toreval left them, re-watching some of the video letters their littermates had sent home after they first left for the Ranger headquarters on Earth for their training period. When Toreval returned, Ilmi was still doing that, alone and shedding tears in silence.

Now, still wrapped up in their parent's arms, Ilmi's eyes have finally dried enough that they're willing to speak again.

"I'm *never* going to be ready for Taldee to leave too," they whisper, their face half-buried against Toreval's shoulder just as their little sibling's was earlier. "Never..."

"Oh, sweetheart," says Toreval, gently stroking their kitten's ears, "I know... I'm not sure if I'll be ready when the time comes either." They sigh softly. "I know this is all hard for you, Ilmi. I'm sorry if today has made it harder."

Ilmi wipes the moisture from their third eye with the back of their hand, finally looking up to meet Toreval's own gaze. "'Hard' doesn't begin to describe it, Nida." They absently begin running the fluff at the tip of their tail through their lower set of fingers. After a long silence, they speak again. "Why... why didn't you tell me?"

"I don't know," Toreval admits. "I suppose I've had a lot on my mind too, lately... and somehow the time just was never right to bring it up." They shake their head lightly. "That's no excuse, I know. I should have been more open with you about what I've been up to and how much I've let your sibling help me."

"Mm... are you going to tell me *now* why Taldee thinks you and this assistant of that woman's are such good friends, then?" There's no acid in their tone, now, only a note of sad resignation.

"Because... well, we are, in a way," Toreval tells them, embarrassed ever so slightly that this is the only answer they can possibly give.

Ilmi looks at them for a few minutes in much the same way they do when Taldee's done something utterly perplexing and kitten-like. "*That's* where you've been all this time? Showing your new 'friend' around the city or something—and out of your robes, too, like you *really* think people won't recognize you and notice who you're with?" Ilmi seems to have at least some of their usual dry sense of humor left, after all.

Toreval nods slowly, doing their best to stifle a chuckle at that last bit. "Well, the disguise is only so the Ensign wouldn't recognize me as an Elder and therefore be more inclined to be candid with me... but yes."

"*Why?*"

"To tell you the truth, Ilmi? Because *I* didn't quite trust Admiral Marvin's intentions when she first came here either. I wanted to get to know her assistant so I could form a better idea of the character of the people we're dealing with for myself—all I had before was what your littermates had told me."

Ilmi gives them a probing glare. "And... you've decided to trust the suspicious military humans now, just because this Ensign fellow is *nice* to you?"

"I'm still deciding," Toreval tells them, gently, "But I do think I trust him, one way or another. He's a better person than you give him credit for... and I haven't seen a kitten yet who wasn't immediately drawn to him." Toreval makes a point of leaving out just how strongly they've found *themself* drawn to the young man. They have a distinct impression that Ilmi wouldn't appreciate hearing about that.

Ilmi hesitates. "Kittens aren't *always* right about people..."

"No, but most of the time their instincts are right on point." Toreval smiles softly. "I think the Ensign might have the potential to be a natural Beacon, actually, although I've not discussed that with anyone but the Eldest yet."

Ilmi raises an eyebrow from their lower pair at Toreval. "I... wouldn't expect that trait in a *warrior*, Nida. Historically, they're usually Artisans of some sort." Their usual aspiring Star-Keeper's curiosity seems to be shining through now, even if it's dimmer than usual.

"He isn't a warrior, dear, even if he does work closely with them." Toreval shrugs. They don't have much else to say on the matter, really, since they *certainly* haven't discussed it with Li yet. "It's just a theory of mine based on my own experiences being around him and some things the different kittens who played with him at the River Festival have told me."

"...I take it Taldee was one of those kittens?"

"Yes, along with the Eldest's Marbree and Myrval... and just about every other kitten around that age who happened to be around." Toreval holds back their amusement remembering the sight of it. "The Ensign is a skilled swimmer and was willing to supervise the kittens whose parents and family adults weren't free to play in the water with them, so he sort of got conscripted into the role. The Eldest supervised *him* as well until they were sure he was sufficient for the task."

"Mm." Ilmi shakes their head lightly. "I'll trust their judgment, then... so what did the kittens have to say about this 'friend' of yours, then?"

"According to your sibling and Marbree, that he was great fun to splash with." Toreval smiles softly, glad at least that Ilmi's curiosity seems to be tempering their other emotions now. "Little Myrval's the one who told me they felt like he may be a Beacon. Apparently his imagination was easy for them to click into, whenever the other kittens got him into playing some bit of make-believe or other with them."

Ilmi nods slowly. "They'd be the one to notice... If he didn't belong to the Admiral, I'd *almost* want to meet him." They make a questioning gesture with their tail. "Are you going to ask the Eldest to test him, then?"

"I don't know, honestly." Toreval shrugs. "I'm waiting to decide *that* until all of the Admiral's business with the Council has concluded."

"I'll be glad when it does." Ilmi rests their head on Toreval's shoulder now with a sigh. "Because once the Council's done debating, she'll *leave*."

"One way or another," Toreval agrees, "she'll need to. She does have a Fleet out there that needs her."

"And her assistant." Ilmi hesitates. "You *know* this 'friend' of yours is going to leave too—and probably get himself killed in this stupid war his people are fighting, if he stays too close to that woman."

"I like to think he has the good sense to stay out of immediate danger if he can," says Toreval, "but yes, I know." They're not sure why they're reluctant, in a way, to think about the day when Li will be leaving.

"And it's... it's *really* just Council business that has you taking him all over the city?"

"I will admit I've enjoyed getting to play tour guide for a change... but yes. Can you accept that? I'd like to continue what I'm doing, at least until the Council comes to its decision."

Ilmi's silent for a long while. Their tail wraps itself around one of Toreval's lower arms, just as it used to when they were a small, insecure kitten needing comforting. Toreval once again begins to lightly stroke their hair in a reassuring way.

"I... don't particularly *like* the idea of you being around one of the Admiral's minions, Nida..." Ilmi begins, then sighs reluctantly. "But I know you must be doing something you think is important, if it's already gone on this long and you haven't lost interest in whatever impulse it was that started it. So I guess I can live with it, as long as you don't expect *me* to spend any amount of time around either him or that woman… and you don't let Taldee be *alone* with her again."

"I can agree to that." Toreval smiles with relief. "Thank you, Ilmi."

The two of them sit there together for a long while after, snuggling just as they have ever since Ilmi and their littermates first came into Toreval's life. The warmth of one's family is the heart of comfort and reassurance, after all. Toreval themself needs that almost as much as their kittens do, especially on days like this.

It's not until Toreval remembers that they *did*, in fact, bring sweet buns and fresh speckle-fruits home to share with their kittens and mentions this to Ilmi that the two of them finally go into the kitchen to see about finding some long-overdue dinner. The rest of the night's conversation stays well away from talk of the Admiral and her assistant or their family's recent losses. Instead, they talk about Ilmi's studies and the star-keeping spheres they're practicing making with the Eldest now that their duties with the River Festival are over.

Toreval regrets, of course, that their kittens have had cause to be upset with each other tonight, but it's been so long since they had a chance like this to spend time alone with Ilmi that in a way they're glad things have worked out that way. Their sweet survivor-smallest is precious to them, more than they could ever explain in words. With how busy the last few weeks have been for both of them, it's nice to enjoy Ilmi's company for a while without anything else pressing on them.

This, after all, is what they want most to protect: their kittens, and the peace of their people's Sanctuary where they have been able to raise them in safety. They never had a choice in becoming a parent, of course, but Toreval has always loved their kittens. They always will.

There will always be a part of them that longs for Iralee and Inayan to still be alive and at their side, and another that dreads the day their youngest will leave them to take on their apprenticeship. Ilmi, they know, has always said they want nothing more than to stay with Toreval in the Sanctuary, and that is some comfort—for otherwise, with no more kittens in their future, Toreval would one day find themself *truly* alone. They could bear it, though, they think, if Ilmi ever found a counterpart who suited them and changed their mind.

So long as their two remaining kittens are happy and safe, Toreval is content.

Now, more than ever, they know they'll do whatever it takes to make sure that Ilmi and Taldee *stay* safe, regardless of what the future holds.

WHEN TOREVAL FIRST ENCOUNTERED LI, he struck them as a very formal, reserved sort of human.

Then again, at the time, he was standing beside Admiral Marvin being introduced to the present members of the Council and listening as she made her initial statement to all of them. There hadn't been any more cause for him to speak than there had for Toreval themself to. Even afterward, when they were first observing him with the Admiral, he still gave them the impression of being quite conscientious and focused solely on his work.

Having gotten to know him better, though, Toreval has come to understand that just like them, Li has a certain way of behaving when he's working. When he's off duty, Li seems far more relaxed in general than he ever did on that first day.

To a certain definition of relaxed, that is.

"You're *sure* we need to climb further? The ground is... kinda far away already."

"You wanted to see the city, Li!" Toreval laughs brightly. "I *promise* you, this view is worth the effort."

"It had better be!"

"You should have told me before we started if you have a problem with heights."

"I don't have a problem with *heights*, Celadon—Just with the idea of hitting the ground when I fall."

Toreval hasn't been to the top of the rock spires on the cliff face overlooking the city in years—not since before Taldee shed their soft silver coat of kitten fur—but the opportunity to make the climb with Li in tow is too good to pass up.

They're aware now that they're growing to appreciate the company of this straightforward young human as a thing in itself beyond any of their initial plans in interacting with him. Li reminds them in many ways of the person they were before their roles as *parent* and *Elder* separated them from the more carefree lives of their older siblings and the explorer's path they'd dreamed of taking. Even if it's only for a short time before the Admiral's business concludes and he leaves, Toreval is glad to have such a friend in their life.

"Ah, not fond of the whims of gravity today? Fair enough." Toreval looks down at him and grins. "We're almost there, though."

Li groans, but with a good-humored tone. "You said that half an hour ago, Celadon."

"Well, perhaps I did at that. But I mean it this time!"

"Oh, sure you do." Li's tone says he's probably rolling his eyes at their back. "What does 'almost there' mean this time? Thirty meters of a sheer cliff face or something?"

"It means almost there!" Laughing again, Toreval catches the last handhold and gracefully flips themself up and on top of the overhang of the stone platform. Once their feet and lower arms are secure, they lean back over the edge to look at Li upside down. They beckon to him with one of their free upper hands. "See? Just the other side of this ledge."

"You *do* realize that move's physically impossible without the extra pair of arms, right?"

"Oh, I'm sure you could manage something. You have the ropes to lean on, after all."

Toreval reaches down with both upper hands and pulls him up anyway. It takes him a few minutes to recover his breath before he looks out over the city.

"*Wow.* Okay, you're right, this is worth the climb."

Toreval nods in agreement. The view from the top of the spire is every bit as beautiful as they remembered.

The entirety of City-on-the-River stretches out below the two of them, spreading from the cliff face and the waterfalls down along the long River itself as a carpet of white domes and terraces spread amidst the purple and black foliage of the continent's largest rainforest. From this high up, even the Council House seems small. On the other end of the valley, the red and white spheres of the suns are just beginning to set over the far edge of the horizon. In an hour or two, the lights of the city will turn on to greet the stars above them.

"So, Li. What do you think?"

"I don't have the words for it just yet..." Li shakes his head lightly, pausing to adjust his climbing harness. "It's amazing, though."

"I'll accept that."

Toreval sits in silence with him, looking out over their home. They remember the first time they brought their eldest kittens to this place to show them to the stars. Toreval's eyes mist over with the memories. Was it really so long ago?

All three of them were so small, then: little more than silver fluffs, all still able to fit in the palms of their hands. Iralee and Inayan scampered all the way up to the tops of the rocks at the back of the ledge, even then excited by the faraway points of light that held their future. Ilmi was the smallest of the litter, barely half the size of their siblings on the day their eyes finally opened—the one who's never strayed far from Toreval's side. Whatever Toreval might have felt in the beginning about the inescapable, painful reality of their own destiny as a parent, they've always treasured their little family.

And now, half of it is gone forever.

"So, Celadon. Why did you bring me up here?" Li's voice draws them back out of the mist of memories.

Toreval shrugs lightly, gesturing out at the city. "I thought you'd appreciate the view."

"Is that all?"

"I was also in a mood to make the climb, if you must know."

"I see." Something in his tone says he's not satisfied with the answer.

"Why *else* would I?"

"I don't know."

"Well, there you go." Toreval begins to absently run the tuft at the end of their tail through their lower pair of hands.

Li shakes his head lightly after a few moments, stifling a laugh. "You're almost as bad as the Admiral, you know?"

"Oh? How so?"

"*Cryptic.* Like you know everything in the world but you're waiting for me to say something specific so you can take it apart."

"Now, why would I want to do something like that?"

"With the Admiral, it's usually because she wants me to figure out something for myself... or to get me into position for something she can't manage outright. With you?" Li shakes his head again and turns his eyes back out towards the sunset. "I have no idea what you want."

Toreval wasn't expecting him to say something like this. It's an interesting development.

"If I knew what I wanted," they say, holding back a sigh, "we wouldn't be having this conversation."

"And there you go again! See? Cryptic."

"Perhaps I am." Toreval chuckles briefly in spite of themself. "Does it matter that much?"

"Probably not in the long run. I'd just rather have everything out on the table to begin with so I can chart a proper course through it, you know?"

"You talk like a Navigator."

"That's what I am—well, what I studied as, at any rate."

"Oh?" Toreval raises one of their eyebrows. In all the conversations they've had with Li since they met him, he's never mentioned this.

"I'm only a T-3/S-8 primary—didn't qualify to go any further than Nav theory and transferred to astral cartography at the Fleet Academy instead once I realized even the best grades I could *possibly* earn wouldn't be enough to convince the administration of Luyten Central to let me into their actual Nav prep program. The Admiral decided she wanted to take me on as her personal assistant because even though the Fleet didn't have any better use for me at the time, I *am* good at memorizing charts and codes... and she likes having someone on hand to translate data from recon and fronts for her without having to put everything through the computers."

"I see."

Li sighs. "But that's neither here nor there. What I was trying to say, *Elder Celadon*, is that if there's something you're trying to get out of me, I'd rather you just get it over with and ask."

Toreval looks over to their human friend, unable to keep themself from laughing. Li is *far* more perceptive than they ever expected. It's oddly refreshing.

"You recognized me immediately, didn't you?"

"You *change clothes*, Celadon. It's hardly a disguise." Li shoots them a brief smirk. "Not to mention that Florivan facial stripes are distinctive... and my memory's essentially photographic for patterns like that."

"I see your point," Toreval concedes, once they've gotten control of their giggles. "Although you'd be surprised how many humans I've encountered who couldn't tell us apart to begin with."

"I've met humans who couldn't tell *other humans* apart."

"Truly? That's odd."

"We're an odd species in general, I'd say."

"No wonder my people were drawn to you."

Li turns to meet their eyes fully and laughs. "Maybe so. Now, how can I help you?"

Toreval holds the gaze of his dark brown, alien eyes for a moment and then looks back out towards the city and the tiered domes of the Council House far below. Somewhere down there, they know, it's about time for Ilmi to catch Taldee and settle them down into their evening lessons. Somewhere also, Li's own mentor is likely beginning to wonder where his 'local guide' has taken him this time that he's not yet returned to give his report.

"What do you think of the Admiral's purpose here?" Toreval asks at last, watching their young human friend's expression closely.

"Why are you asking *me*?"

"You have a perspective on the situation. I'd like to know what it is."

"I don't see why."

"You and I are alike in a way. To use your phrasing, I want to have more information out on the table. I've gotten all I can from your Admiral, and now I want to know what her young assistant thinks of the situation."

"Ah. I'm not exactly qualified as a tactician..."

"You don't have to be." Toreval can't help thinking that despite his hesitation, he's more adept at such things than he lets on. Their interactions with the Admiral have shown them that she thinks highly of him, at least—far more than someone like her would if he was really nothing more than a loyal subordinate.

Li takes a long breath and then lets it out audibly. "You *do* know I'm going to have to tell her you asked?"

"I *expect* that you will, yes."

"Okay, then." Li falls silent for a while, staring out at the city and the growing colors of the sunset.

Toreval watches his body language closely. There's an air of almost decisive calmness about him that they can't help but find compelling.

"I think she's right, of course," Li says at last. "Our ships are too slow, even with the best engines we've designed. The Novans can outrun us coming and going—even if our darter pilots are better than their strikers in a dogfight, they can still get in or out of attack range before we can do anything about it. When they get around to mounting a large-scale assault on our systems, we'll likely be overrun in a matter of weeks."

Li picks up a rough grey and black pebble from the loose stones behind them and begins silently turning it over in his hand.

Toreval suspects the young human has more to say, so they wait patiently for him to collect his words and continue.

"Not to mention," Li says at last, "that the Alliance folks are spread too thin fighting their big war to really do much to help us, and they have too many restrictions about what kind of help they can give even though *they're* mostly to blame for us being caught in this nonsense." He pauses to shake his head, still turning the pebble over in his hand. "The only way the Fleet can hope to stand up to *anyone* in the long term is with QSD tech—and we can't have that without your cooperation, since no amount of lenses and shielding is ever going to be enough to make it safe for humans to work in contact Quantum Space like Florivans can."

Toreval nods. He's right, of course, particularly on that last point. It took the better part of a decade from when their people first became friends with his young, inquisitive species to adapt their way of traveling the stars so they could safely share it. It took even longer for the sort of interstellar ships like the one they themself apprenticed on to be well-developed enough to become as commonplace as they now are.

"I'm familiar with the Alliance members' reasons for withholding things, but in our case..." Toreval pauses, choosing their words carefully. "Humans are our *friends*. We Florivans like sharing the stars with you. That's why we've shared as much of our technology with you as we have, because we want to be fully a part of the world our peoples have begun to create together." There's more to it than that, of course, but they don't see a need to be overly detailed at the moment.

"And at the same time," Li counters, "Drive tech has never been approved for military service. If I remember right from what the Admiral's Rangers told me, the only reason their sort get an exception is because they're *peacekeepers*, rather than warriors—and there's not many of them out there to begin with. Is that right?"

"To put it simply, yes." Toreval nods. "Not many of us take that path, but those who do are seen as dedicating their lives to helping keep your people from repeating some of the more... *unpleasant*... aspects of your history—

that's why even the most cautious members of the Council don't usually argue against it."

Toreval looks down to their hands for a few moments, trying to clear the memory of the arguments they had with their parent on the subject back when Iralee and Inayan first finished their apprenticeships and informed the family of the path both of them had chosen. Toreval knows the latest version of that argument was fueled by grief on both sides, but that doesn't make it hurt less—nor the fact that their parent hasn't spoken to them since.

Li's voice cuts through the silence and the pangs of the memories once again.

"I'm sorry, Celadon. I shouldn't have brought that up, should I? I'd imagine that's still a fresh wound for you."

"Hmm?" It takes them a moment to realize that *of course* Li would have connected the dots by now, perceptive human that he is. He's the Admiral's most trusted assistant; *he'd* have been the one processing the information from her scouts. "Oh. Yes, a bit—but I'm fine, really. You were saying?"

Li looks at them in a way that says he's not entirely sure that they *are* fine, then sighs and gestures vaguely towards the sunset. "What I was *trying* to say is that if we want to protect our systems from the Novans—Procyon included— what other option *is* there? We couldn't demand anything from you, of course, and I *still* don't see how your Council would ever agree to openly just... send people with us. But if we *could* have even a handful of jumpers in the Fleet?" Li makes a vague gesture towards the sky. "I wager they'd make all the difference."

"The Council might disagree with that on principle."

"Well, naturally. We're asking your people to step up and help us fight a war none of us wanted to be involved in in the first place. Even though you'd only be helping us get around, I can see how the *idea* of it would rub the wrong way."

"That's something of an understatement," Toreval tells him, holding back a sigh of their own. "Some of the oldest members of the Council were raised by people with living memory of when we came to Procyon—witnesses to the oaths our ancestors swore when they built all of this. That holds a lot of sway over how we conduct things, even today." Toreval is all too familiar with the old stories and traditions. They spent the majority of their kittenhood in the care of the Council's Eldest, after all, a person who, like Toreval's actual parent, is a member of only the third generation of Elders raised in the Sanctuary here.

"Really?" Li turns to them with a curious tilt of his head. "I didn't know that Florivans weren't native to this system."

"We aren't native to any system, really," Toreval says simply, not wanting to change the course of the conversation too much. "It's not something we discuss often."

"So why tell me?"

"Why do you think?"

"You're being cryptic again, Celadon."

"Am I?"

"Definitely."

Toreval looks up to the stars that they can feel are starting to shine out above them, then down to the lights of the city shining over the domes. It takes them a few moments to find the right words, but it feels *important* somehow that they try to explain things to this young human friend of theirs.

"This planet is the only home I have ever known, Li," they say at last. "It sits between the warmth of the Strange and the peace of the Stars, my people's Sanctuary from millennia of wandering unwanted by anyone in search of something... indescribable. Your people are the friends we've chosen to tie our path to, and would be our *anchor.* I have no doubt that if you are at risk, we shall be as well."

"I'm not sure I understand entirely..."

"You don't have to."

"You agree with us, though?" Li gives them a particularly curious look. "That the Novans are a threat to your people too?"

"I think they could be," Toreval admits. "Regardless of what the rest of the Council decides... *I* will give my life if it means protecting all of this, just as I would have given it for the sake of my kittens."

"Then you're going to support us?"

Toreval stays silent for a long while, there on the spire between the city and the stars. That's the question they've been asking themself ever since Li and the Admiral he serves first arrived. That was their purpose in getting to know Li, after all, to help them find the answers that couldn't be found within their own mind. This conversation with him has been a long time coming, and it *has* been worth the trouble. Between his consideration and the talks they've had with Navy over their relay-letters and Elder Caeruleus and the others who've come in from the stars since, there's no denying what Toreval themself now believes is the right course of action.

Finally, they look back to their human friend with a sigh.

"I will do what I can, yes. I'm still the Youngest among our Elders, you know. It remains to be seen whether my support will carry any weight."

"Every little bit helps, I suppose." Li shrugs lightly. "I'm sure the Admiral will be happy to know that you're on our side after all."

"Perhaps."

"Speaking of the Admiral..." Li leans to look over the edge of the stone the two of them are perched upon. "Is there an easier way down from here? I doubt she would be happy about me staying up here all night."

Toreval can't help chuckling. There's something in his change of tones that settles the emotions the conversation has brought up in them, at least for the moment.

"Now, Li, *really*! Where's your sense of adventure?"

"On the ground, at the moment." Li rolls his eyes at them, then lets out a small laugh.

"Well, think of it this way: 'down' is far easier to accomplish than 'up'!"

While they help their human friend rappel down, Toreval decides that they were right to follow their initial impulse to seek him out. Li is an interesting sort; well worth continuing to keep as a friend for as long as they can, even though they now know everything they need in order to make their decision.

Part 3: The Choices We Make

ALMOST A MONTH AFTER THE ADMIRAL FIRST arrived with her request, and the day after Toreval climbed the spires with Li, the last two spacefaring Elders finally arrive and the Council meets in full.

The discussion of the matter takes up most of another week.

For their part, Toreval is surprised it doesn't take longer, with almost three hundred Elders gathered and arguing about *everything*. There's a reason the whole Council is only called to meet in person for serious issues, after all. Ordinary business that requires the full Council's input can be handled via relay correspondence, too. Most of the time, it's just the partial body that takes care of everyday matters at the Council House: the Eldest, whatever twelve Elders are on the duty rotation that season, perhaps three or four others who happen to be involved with some specific issue, and the Youngest.

In the seven years since Toreval was named to the latter position, and even before that when they were only a new parent and destined Elder apprenticed to the Eldest, they've *never* seen an issue come up that was serious enough to call in the full Council.

Toreval spends most of their time during the deliberations quietly encouraging those whom they can to side with the humans and helping the voices of the Elders like Caeruleus and their old mentor Azul who've come in from the stars with their Navigators to be heard. Toreval knows that those are their best hope for gaining support, since they're more personally familiar with the details of human society and the galactic situation than the rest of the Council. The traditions binding Elders mean that a large majority of those gathered to make this decision have seldom left the sanctuary of their system, if ever. Exceptions to the rule like Caeruleus and Azul are rare, but they've begun to grow more common in recent years; a total of seven partnered Elders have had to divert their starships to Procyon for this meeting.

It's not Toreval's role to openly argue for either position, though. As the Youngest, they can't speak out until *after* the Council has come to a decision, just as the Eldest is required to remain a neutral party in a full session like this and act solely as the voice and will of the Council. All either of them can do, for now, is listen and wait.

Finally, the day comes when all of the talking is over and the silent votes have been cast.

Toreval is sitting high on the uppermost balcony on the far side of the wide Council Hall to observe the proceedings, just as they have since the session opened. Their presence isn't required down on the ground in the center of everything as the Eldest's is; they'd been tasked with *watching* and *listening* in the opening ceremony, and this is their preferred vantage point. Beside them on one side is their beloved former mentor Elder Azul, while Elder Celeste, their predecessor as Youngest and another of the star-jumping exceptions to the rules binding Elders to the Sanctuary, sits on the other. The Navigators belonging to both their friends and all the others who have accompanied their Elder counterparts are not present; the seven of them are all out in the waiting area outside the Council Hall, just as they have been all week.

The only humans in the room are Admiral Marvin and Li. Both of them are dressed in their most formal Defense Fleet uniforms and standing on the dais below opposite the place of honor where the Eldest and the other most senior members of the Council are seated. The time has finally come for the Eldest to pronounce the Council's verdict.

Even though it's unlikely anyone would chance to look up at them, and Elders Azul and Celeste are hardly the sort to judge them for their nervousness to begin with, Toreval is glad that their tail is concealed by all of the layers of amber silk in their robes. Otherwise, the agitated swishing motions they can't seem to stop it from making would be far harder to conceal.

"We have heard your request, Admiral Marvin, and we have considered the issue you bring before us at great length," the Eldest says, still sitting in their place of honor at the head of the Council with their lower pair of hands resting on the head of their ornately-carved wooden cane. They gesture widely around the room with one of their upper hands as they continue to speak, the translucent white silks of their sleeves fluttering softly. "With the consensus of a majority of the Elders gathered here, it is the decision of this Council..."

The Eldest pauses, raising both upper hands now to gesture to the rings of balconies around the hall where all of the gathered Elders are seated, and to the places of honor at their sides where the other four most senior Elders sit. This is a pointed part of the rituals of the Council, meant to signify the unity of their people regardless of what decision has been made—although Toreval has spent enough of their life now in the Eldest's company to know that they *always* go through the rituals and proclamations more slowly when they want to make certain that everyone is paying attention.

That knowledge does nothing to make the tip of Toreval's tail stop twitching erratically, though, while they wait for the Eldest to finish giving the declaration.

"...That we *cannot* be party to such acts of aggression and violence as the participation of our people in your war would allow."

Toreval can't believe their ears at first.

They were *sure* that at least half of the gathered Elders had understood the implications of the Admiral's words before the votes were taken. They've been encouraged by the testimonies, too. Even some of the people they least expected have spoken up in support of the humans' cause.

They thought that the Council would actually agree.

They were wrong.

They *have* to do something.

"Therefore, Admiral Marvin," the Eldest continues, still speaking slowly and methodically, "on behalf of this Council and the Florivan people as a whole, we ask—"

"—Please!" Toreval shouts, all four hands tightly gripping the railing in front of them as they stand up for the sake of their kittens. "Don't make this mistake, Eldest."

A murmur of shocked voices echoes around the Council Hall.

"Sit down, Toreval!" This demand from the person in pale yellow robes sitting near the Eldest's side stings more than any other could. Somehow, despite all of the arguments the two of them have had over the years, Toreval still held the hope that their parent would understand.

Toreval *doesn't* sit down, though.

Instead, they slip over the railing in front of them with a practiced ease. They land on the chamber floor with a light thud and a flutter of amber silk as their robes catch the air. The murmurs drop into a stunned silence.

In a few short steps, Toreval has joined the humans on the dais.

"The Council has *already* heard from those opposed to this decision, Toreval!" Their parent narrows all three eyes at them briefly, as if they're nothing more than a naughty kitten in need of scolding. "Go back to your seat before you embarrass this Council any further."

"The Council has not heard from *me*." Toreval pointedly ignores the custom of formal address, just as their parent has. "It is my *duty* as Youngest to speak out when the wisdom of the Council is in error."

"What else is there to say?" Their parent waves their upper-right hand dismissively. "We cannot allow our people to be used—"

"—We cannot allow innocents to die needlessly from our inaction!"

"*Toreval*!"

Toreval looks away from the disapproving eyes of their parent, focusing instead on the Eldest. They steel themself and shift their tone to the calmest, most respectful one they have. "*Please*, Eldest. Allow me the chance to beg this Council to reconsider."

The Eldest fixes them with a questioning gaze and then a long, slow blink of all three golden eyes at once. Toreval can't immediately tell if that's meant as a gesture of reassurance or disapproval.

"When we named you an Elder, Celadon Toreval, we charged you with the Youngest's task." The Eldest raises an eyebrow and gestures briefly to Toreval with the tip of their cane for emphasis. "We did not expect you to use it so recklessly."

"Forgive me, Eldest, for being so abrupt." Toreval speaks with polite earnestness. "I had *thought* the Council would have clear eyes in this matter even without my words."

"In accordance with your role," the Eldest says, dipping their head slightly, "we must allow you to speak. Let the Council turn our ears to our Youngest!" The Eldest taps the stone of the floor with the tip of their cane, marking this as official.

Toreval folds all four hands together in a gesture of respectful gratitude, then takes in a long, slow breath and addresses the Council.

"I speak as the Youngest of the Council: the watcher, the listener, the one who speaks for those who cannot. I speak on behalf of your kittens and mine, for the Eldest holds our people's past and the Council keeps our present, but it is the Youngest's task to guard our *future*."

Toreval recites the words of the ancient ritual calmly and precisely. This is something they never thought they'd actually have to do, but they're prepared. The Eldest and their predecessor as Youngest *both* drilled them in all of the ritual forms and duties from the day they were brought back to Procyon from their apprenticeship as a destined Elder. A glance up to the balcony where Elders Celeste and Azul are still sitting rewards them with a pair of reassuring nods. Their predecessor and former mentor, at least, both seem to still approve of them.

"Without our help," Toreval continues, "this war that our friends have been brought into will either see them destroyed outright or it will drag on endlessly until their systems are too weak to remain unconquered. We will not become weapons or soldiers; the humans *know* this and they have always respected it. But if we help them now, we can give them a chance to survive at least!"

"You say nothing that has not been said before, Youngest," Elder Caeruleus notes from their seat on the other side of the Eldest from Toreval's parent—understandably, considering that this is the person who made that particular point during the Council's first day of deliberations. "Is this the extent of the wisdom you offer us?"

"If I repeat what has been said, Elder Caeruleus," Toreval replies, dipping their head respectfully, "I do so because they are words which bear *truths* this Council has chosen to ignore."

Elder Caeruleus nods to them with an encouraging flick of their ears.

Toreval turns their eyes back to the rest of the room. "And while I am repeating the wisdom I have heard in this hall, let me say this again too: Our people *will* become part of this conflict even if we attempt to avoid it! It is only a matter of time. All of our people who jump stars with their Navigators are *already* at risk!" They raise a hand in a sweeping gesture toward the section of the upper galleries where they know the majority of the spacefaring Elders are sitting. Toreval knows for sure that the emphasis for this point will not be lost there. "Even if they do not become part of the human Defense Fleet as the Admiral has described, the Novan Imperium will *not* show them mercy any more than they do to our human friends—"

"—Even so, Toreval, you're exaggerating the risk!" Toreval wishes it was anyone else, but it's their parent again who interrupts now to lead the arguments against them. "We cannot allow—"

"—Will we allow the Novans to come for *us*, then, when they have finished with our friends and we have no protection left?" Toreval asks the Council, trying to turn their eyes away from the disappointed gaze their parent has fixed on them. "The human colony at Luyten's Star lies only a single light-year away. Almost a *thousand* of our people live there at the North City Sanctuary, in the place that the humans there gave to us when we first became their friends—as do twelve of the Elders who sit here among us! Are we to trust that the Novans will treat our people at Luyten's Star *kindly*, when they are a part of the human colony there? More than that, is this Council so short-sighted as to think our Sanctuary *here* will be overlooked if—no, *when*—the Luyten's Star colony falls?"

"Toreval!" their parent shouts again, "*Enough*! You may be the Youngest, but that does not give you free rein to insult this Council. If you truly had the best for our people in mind, you would be *silent* and let those with more experience make this decision—as we *already have*!"

Something deep in Toreval's being snaps when they hear this. Any appearance of calm consideration they might have been projecting disappears in an instant. Their tail swishes with agitation beneath their robes.

"I will *not* be silent when two of my kittens have already given their lives to protect us!"

Judging from the loud murmurs that now fill the Council Hall, very few, if any, of the gathered Elders were aware of the connection. Toreval themself hasn't shared the true details of their family's recent loss with anyone but Ilmi, of course, out of respect for the secrecy under which their kittens were working—but the Admiral had been honest about what *happened* to the two Ranger pairs who had unofficially joined her command when she made her speech to the Council. She was equally honest about the fact that open assistance would mean giving up Procyon's protected status, which sparked no end of arguments in itself.

It only takes a moment for Toreval's parent to turn the shocked look of realization on their face into one of angered disappointment. "Then you mean their *counterparts* pledged their lives—"

"—No, I *do not*!" Toreval takes a moment to draw in a deep centering breath before they explain, trying to pull their own tone back to earnest calmness. "Volunteering to serve as scouts was my Teal's idea. Turquoise agreed with them. *Both* consulted me before they ever made the offer to the Admiral. They believed they had a duty to our people as much as to their anchors. They *knew* what was at stake for all of us, Florivan and human alike, when the greater powers in this galaxy set their eyes towards the human systems!"

Toreval had hoped all of this would go more smoothly, but here it is—all out on the table, as Li would say.

"Then it is your *own* failing as a parent you admit before us all, Toreval! You allowed them to go against everything this Council stands for—just as you are now!" Toreval's parent hisses. "You should *never* have allowed those two to go off with those so-called 'peacekeepers' in the first place—"

"—I allowed them to do what they felt was right!" Toreval raises their voice to be heard over the din of murmurs and outraged voices in the balconies. "And I stand by what Teal and Turquoise believed in! They *chose* to help our friends. They *chose* to do what they could within the limits of our nature to protect our people. Now *I* stand before you all on their behalf, to ask that you give the same choice to our people. We give our kittens the freedom to choose their counterparts and their paths in this life—we give them the choice to leave this Sanctuary *freely*! It should be *their* choice to help our friends protect it as well."

The Eldest raises both upper hands to quiet the growing commotion of arguing among the other Elders. It takes several loud taps of their cane against the floor to call everyone back to some semblance of order.

When the Eldest is finally satisfied with the silence in the room, they turn to Toreval's parent with a calm but firm cast to their eyes. "Elder Lazurite, we understand that you have a standing disagreement with the Youngest regarding these matters?"

"That is a bit of an understatement, Eldest, but yes," their parent says flatly, still aiming a disappointed expression of their own at Toreval. "I apologize for the disruption they seem *determined* to cause to these proceedings."

"The Council will accept an apology for your *own* behavior, nothing more." The Eldest's ears twitch now in a way that says they're either amused or disappointed, or possibly a bit of both—although Toreval can't say for sure now *who* those feelings would be aimed at.

"Eldest?" asks their parent, taken aback.

"We must remind you, Elder Lazurite..." the Eldest begins, gesturing broadly with one hand, "...that all members of this Council are *equals* sharing in the burdens of our kind and the leadership of our people." The Eldest points the tip of their cane at Toreval for emphasis. "We must therefore *also* remind you that your responsibility for Celadon Toreval's behavior ended the day they were named an Elder—as did your authority over them."

"I..." Toreval's parent hesitates and then lets out a frustrated sigh. "I stand reminded, Eldest."

"Good. If the two of you wish to argue further, we would thank you to do so in private. When you are before the Council, you *will* treat each other with the respect due to fellow Elders. Do you both understand this?"

"...Yes, Eldest."

"Yes, Eldest," Toreval echoes.

"Good. Now that *that* has been dealt with..." The Eldest taps their cane on the floor again. "...We may return to our proceedings."

Toreval's parent deflates a bit and leans back in their chair, shaking their head.

Toreval has to wonder if their parent is as embarrassed as they are to have been reprimanded like this in front of the entire Council and the two human guests—but at the same time, they can't help but be grateful that the Eldest said something at all.

"You do seem to have a lot to say to us now that the votes have been cast, Youngest..." The Eldest pauses in the silence for a painfully long moment and fixes Toreval with an ancient, piercing look once more, then softens ever so slightly. "...But it is your *role* to challenge this Council when our collective wisdom may be in error or tradition may blind us to danger."

Toreval dips their head respectfully, grateful at least that the Eldest has not stopped them from speaking.

"So, Youngest... have you now said all that you feel you must?"

"I have, Eldest."

"You would have us leave it up to our kittens to decide whether to stay here in the safety of the Sanctuary with us..." The Eldest gestures vaguely with one upper hand, returning to their slow, formal way of speaking. "...Or to follow yours on a path which would not only contribute to violence, but that would likely lead to their own deaths. Tell me, Youngest: do you *truly* understand the implications of what you are asking of this Council?"

Toreval takes a moment in the silence to focus themself. They have to stand firm on this. "Yes, Eldest, I believe I do—and I will be the first to take that path, if it has the chance of protecting our people and our friends from a destruction which is *unavoidable* if we do nothing."

"Oh, will you, now?" The Eldest raises all three eyebrows.

There's one last move Toreval can make to convince the other Elders, and they know it's impulsive—but what other choice do they have? It's the only thing they can think of that might prove their point. They only hope it will be enough.

"I have chosen my Navigator, Eldest." Toreval gestures with both left hands to the place behind them where the two humans are still standing. "*Regardless* of what this Council decides, I will be leaving the Sanctuary to aid the Admiral's cause."

The murmurs and arguing overtake the hall again for a good ten minutes until the Eldest finally has any success in silencing everyone again. Once the commotion has died down, the Eldest gestures to the Admiral with their cane.

"Is this *true*, Admiral Marvin?" the Eldest asks, all three ancient golden eyes intensely focused on the woman standing behind Toreval. "Has our Youngest indeed pledged themself to your service?"

"It's news to me too, Eldest," the Admiral replies, calmly, "but I assure you, I will *gladly* accept Elder Celadon and their Navigator's service as the new Quantum Space Drive team for my flagship—and, for that matter, as my official Florivan advisor and the overseer of any others of your people who would volunteer their services to the Defense Fleet."

"I see. Very well, then..." The Eldest taps the floor with their cane several times to settle some stray murmurs and then gestures with it towards the great carved doors of the Council Hall. "You may go and wait in the outer rooms until you are called for, Admiral Marvin. It seems we will need to deliberate further in order to bring this matter to conclusion."

The Admiral bows elegantly. "I thank the Council for reconsidering."

Toreval turns and watches as the Admiral and Li step off the dais. The humans have only gone a few steps towards the doors before the Eldest speaks again.

"Go with your Navigator, Youngest."

"Eldest?"

"The Council has heard your views and will consider what you have said... but *you* have made your choice. Abide by it."

"...Yes, Eldest."

Toreval follows the humans out, forcing themself not to look back at the Council even once the doors have fully shut behind them.

★

ALMOST HALF AN HOUR LATER, ADMIRAL MARVIN is still pacing between the door of the same small sitting room where she was waiting when Toreval first spoke to her and the balcony overlooking the courtyard. She's been silent ever since they left the Council Hall. Whatever emotions she's feeling are being channeled solely into the motion of her feet as she walks back and forth across the room.

Taldee was sitting in the hallway interviewing Navigators for their continued assignment studying visiting humans when the three of them emerged from the Council chamber. The kitten has now made a game of sorts of following a few steps behind the Admiral's path. The Admiral, for her part, seems to be lost in thought enough that she doesn't seem to have noticed them yet.

Toreval watches the little parade from one of the seats nearer to the door, glad at least that their youngest kitten is still in high spirits. For their own part, the adrenaline which fueled their stand before the Council has worn off entirely. All that's left is exhausted apprehension.

"You know, Youngest," the Admiral says at last with a frustrated sigh as she passes by Toreval again, "it would have been *helpful* if you'd *warned* me you were planning to do that."

"You'll have to forgive me, Admiral." Toreval sighs, smoothing the wrinkles out of one of the layers of amber silk draped over their folded legs with their lower pair of hands. Their upper pair of arms remain loosely crossed over their chest. "I wasn't expecting that I would need to make a final stand for your cause today."

"Let's just hope your little gamble pays off." Admiral Marvin shakes her head as she passes by again. "*Especially* since you've effectively forced me into reassigning my assistant. Do you know how long it took me to find a suitable one?"

"I have a vague idea..." Toreval trails off. The Admiral is using the same tone of voice on them now that Indigo used to use when they'd caused just a shade too much trouble as a kitten. If it weren't for their lingering nerves about the whole situation, they'd almost be amused by that.

"It's not going to be easy to find someone to replace him, that's for sure."

"I'd imagine not."

"Wait—you're reassigning me?" Li looks up from whatever it is he's been reading and typing up on his pocket-com since he sat down on the chair opposite the couch Toreval is sitting on.

The Admiral finally stops pacing long enough to look over between Toreval and Li. Taldee, not expecting her to stop, runs into her legs. She almost loses her balance for a moment from the impact. Her composure regained, she laughs and briefly pats Taldee on the shoulder as a seeming gesture of apology for causing the collision, then turns back to Toreval.

"You didn't warn *him* either, did you?"

Toreval turns their eyes over towards Li. He *does* seem incredibly confused. "I... haven't had much of a chance to discuss it with him, as yet, to be fair."

"You are the *strangest* Florivan I've ever met, Celadon Toreval." The Admiral shakes her head again. She seems to have regained some of the good humor Toreval has come to expect from her. "You know that?"

"I will take that as a compliment, Admiral."

"You should." The Admiral chuckles. "Now, why don't I take Lapis here down to the courtyard for some fresh air and a snack of some sort while you explain to the Ensign just exactly what you did in there?"

"Thank you, Admiral. We'll call down if the Council sends someone out for us before you return." Toreval nods gratefully, then looks to their kitten. "Lapis? Why don't you see if any of the Navigators will go with you and take Admiral Marvin to your Entile Indigo's? I'm sure there's some of *them* who'd appreciate a chance to get some snacks too. You can stay there with Indigo and Monica until I'm done with the rest of the Council business."

"Yes, Nida!" Taldee has enough of an imprint on both humans by now that they don't hesitate at all to go with the Admiral—and, in fact, excitedly take her hand and start asking her what sort of native fruit juices she hasn't tried yet. Toreval has no doubt that their youngest will be quick to find their own Navigator when the time comes, judging by how swiftly they seem to latch on to humans in general.

Li looks over to them once the door has closed, still wearing a rather confused expression. "What was she talking about, Celadon?"

Toreval takes a moment to choose their words carefully. "In my bid to win the Council to our cause," they say at last, "I'm afraid I've put you into something of a... difficult position."

"You're coming with us; that much I understood." Li continues fixing them with a confused, but curious gaze as he slips his deactivated pocket-com back into his pocket. "Now, put the rest of it out on the table for me, will you? Because that whole exchange in there and just now is at *least* five different shades of cryptic already."

"I told the Eldest that I'd chosen my Navigator."

"Okay, I heard that part, yes. And it riled up all the other Elders when you said it—which was one of the things that I didn't understand."

"It's... well, somewhat taboo for one of us to choose a counterpart after being named Elder—or even after being recognized as someone who will *become* an Elder one day, for that matter." Toreval lets out a small sigh, pushing away the unbidden thoughts of the things they had to give up when they were identified as a reproductive individual.

"It's considered too dangerous a lifestyle for an Elder to take part in, essentially."

Li arches an eyebrow at them. "I thought the whole reason we had to wait so long was because some of the folks in there had to jump in from other systems?"

"They all either live at Luyten's Star or had become Elders long after making their compacts. It's a different situation entirely in both cases."

"I don't see why."

Toreval pauses, folding all four hands together in their lap. They don't know where to even begin to explain all of the context and nuances to him—they're not even sure a human would be *able* to comprehend the complex intersections of biology and culture involved. They settle for a simpler answer that will easily redirect the conversation back to the thing they actually *need* to talk about right now.

"What you need to understand right now is that what I've done goes against several of our most important traditions—things I swore to stand by when I was named to the Council."

"That explains why they asked you to leave with us, I guess." Li shrugs, then gives them yet another curious expression. "So you're in some sort of Elder's time out now because you broke one of their rules?"

"You... could put it that way, yes." Toreval sighs. "But I *don't* regret breaking it. The public declaration of my Navigator was my best option for proving I was serious about this. If nothing else, the Fleet will have *one* ship with the Drive now."

"Ah. I still don't see what that has to do with…" Li trails off, his dark brown eyes widening until Toreval can see the fullness of the white parts. "Oh."

"I… *did* strongly indicate that you were my choice, yes."

Li rubs awkwardly at the bridge of his nose for a moment before gesturing vaguely with the same hand. "You *know* I'm not assessed high enough to be anything more than a glorified map-reader, right?"

"I think there's more to you than your letters," Toreval tells him. "Besides, managing maps and star charts is only half of the job, really."

"And the other half?"

"To put it simply?" Toreval chuckles. "Keeping me out of trouble."

"If that's the job, I can already tell I'll have my hands full—at least if what you pulled in there is any indication. I can *see* where Lapis gets that sparky impulsive streak, now."

Toreval glances down at their folded hands. Li has a point, of course. Toreval knows they're asking him to take on a burden even beyond what most Navigators will ever have to carry. They should have talked to him about the possibility before now.

They should have realized how much they *wanted* it to be a possibility before they were standing in front of the Council.

"You are allowed to turn this down, Li." Toreval unfolds their lower-left hand from the rest and smooths another wrinkle out of the silks laying over their legs, then looks back to their human friend with a sigh. "It's not a commitment anyone should take on lightly… or under pressure of the kind I've just put on you. I apologize for that."

Li is silent for a long moment, then tilts his head to one side curiously. "It's more than just a job, then?"

"It is," Toreval admits, trying to find the right words to explain. "The job alone means putting our lives in each other's hands with every jump. Without a certain level of trust, it's almost impossible to do the work at all. The compact between a Florivan and their counterpart is usually a partnership we choose for life—friendship as dear as family, you could call it. Both in and out of the Strange, you'd become my anchor... and I'd be by your side through all things, as long as you'd let me."

Li rubs absently at his temple with one hand. "That explains *so* much about the Nav folks I've run into."

"I'm sure it does."

"And you've quite literally jumped into this to prove a point, when you barely even know me." Li looks to them with an incredulous gaze that matches the almost exasperated tone in his voice.

"You... could put it that way, yes. I feel I've learned enough about your character and abilities to be content with the choice." Toreval hesitates for a moment. "I *do* consider you a dear friend, Li... if taking a counterpart had *been* an option for me before today, I would have probably asked you anyway, sooner or later."

"It's been what, Celadon, a month?" Li shakes his head, letting out a single astonished laugh. "That's not time enough to get to know *anyone*—and now you're saying we're going to be stuck with each other *forever*?"

Toreval hesitates again. They don't know how to explain the reality of the situation any better than they already have. They also don't know how to properly explain that the last month was all they needed to form the beginnings of a strong imprint on him.

They like this young human more than any other they've ever encountered; they feel at ease in his presence in a way they haven't with anyone since they were a kitten. Li is interesting and perceptive and has an oddly reassuring air around him that they can't help but find fascinating. He has a nice sort of bright, even-toned voice that Toreval *knows* would carry well in the Strange, too. With his incredible memory and talent for starcharts and codes considered as well, Li will be an excellent Navigator once he's properly trained—they're *certain* of that.

"As I said, Li," Toreval says at last, "it's your right to say no. I won't fault you for it."

Li raises his eyebrows at them. "What happens with your Council if I do?"

"I don't know. I'll... oh, I'll think of something."

Toreval stands and walks over to the balcony to look out at the courtyard, unable to meet his eyes any longer. They honestly *don't* know what would happen. The thought of it is troubling. If the declaration was enough to sway the Elders, then having their chosen Navigator reject them could unravel everything. Everything they've done would be for *nothing*, then.

Somewhere, deep under all of the other things on their mind, the thought registers that the idea of losing the friendship they've formed with Li—of the possibility of seeing him leave for the stars *without them*—is accompanied by a unique and unexpected twinge of pain.

A long silence, and then Li is standing beside them. When Toreval looks up, he's smiling softly.

"So... is there an oath I'm supposed to take now, or what?"

"Nothing that formal." Toreval is nearly overwhelmed by the wave of relief that washes over them now. "It's just a statement of some sort from each of us acknowledging the arrangement in front of a family member—the Admiral would count too, in your case. I've done my half of that now, technically... but you don't have to say anything to anyone unless you're sure you want to be stuck with me."

"I shouldn't have put it that way."

"It's true, though."

Li leans against the railing beside them and chuckles—this time with no trace of awkwardness in his tone. "Well, Celadon, my friend... at least you're going to be an interesting person to be stuck with."

Toreval finds themself smiling and wishing their friend was the sort of human who liked being touched, because the impulse to hug him is so strong. They settle for lightly nudging him with one of their lower elbows instead.

"I could say the same about you, Li."

★

It only takes four hours for the Council to call them all back, in the end.

Toreval is surprised it doesn't take longer, and they're uncertain whether the short interval bodes well. One way or another, they know they can't do anything more to change the Council's collective mind now.

Toreval walks into the Council Hall and stands on the dais between their Navigator and the Admiral. And Li *is* their Navigator now—he said as much when the Admiral returned to the waiting chamber.

That had surprised Toreval, too. They somehow expected Li would need more time to decide whether or not to reject them. They will have to be sure not to underestimate his ability to adapt to unexpected situations again.

Toreval folds both sets of hands together, upper in front, lower behind. They can feel all of the eyes from the Elders staring at them as they enter—all but their parent, who pointedly looks away. They expected as much, but expectation does not make it sting any less.

The Eldest stands this time, leaning on their cane and gesturing broadly with their upper hands to quiet the room. That done, they hold one of their upper hands out towards the dais.

"Admiral Jennifer Marvin of the Sol Coalition Defense Fleet, you stand before this Council once again... Are you prepared this time to abide by our decision without question?"

The Admiral takes a step forward. "I am, Eldest."

"Very well. The Council has chosen..." The Eldest takes an even longer pause than usual.

Toreval stands there trying to appear as calm and composed as they can, grateful that the layers of their robes hide the anxious twitching motions of their tail. They wrap the end of the appendage around one leg just in case.

"...To stand by our earlier decision. We will *not* be encouraging our people to become involved in your war at this time, and we ask that you not recruit openly for your cause."

Toreval's breath catches in their throat. They can't believe it. They were *so* sure that the rest of the Elders would see reason. The only thing that keeps them from stepping forward immediately to protest is the unfamiliar but welcome warmth of their Navigator subtly reaching over to briefly set a hand on the elbow of their lower arm closest to him. They know Li's meaning to remind them that they promised the Admiral they wouldn't cause any more disturbances without warning. They focus their lower two eyes on the pattern of the floor tiles, steadying their breathing.

The Admiral, for her part, does not betray any emotion by her posture. She simply makes a polite nod to the Eldest. "I understand, Eldest, and I thank the Council for their consideration—"

"—However..."

"However?" the Admiral echoes.

"*However*," the Eldest says again, "as our wayward Youngest has brought to our attention... it is not the way of our people to deny the freedom of choice to our grown kittens, even when we might disagree with their choices."

Toreval's eyes flick up to meet those of the Eldest, who has now placed all four hands on the carved head of their cane and makes an almost imperceptible nod in their direction.

"Therefore, if any more of our people choose of their own accord to *volunteer* to serve on your vessels with a full understanding of the dangers and consequences they may face as a result of foregoing their status as a member of a Neutral and Protected species... the members of this Council have agreed that we will *not* deny them that choice."

A wave of relief washes over Toreval. They couldn't have asked for a better response, given the circumstances. A glance of their third eye to the Eldest's side tells them that this concession was not something their parent supported at all—not that that's surprising.

"I understand, Eldest. Thank you."

"You may leave us now, Admiral Marvin." The Eldest makes a brief gesture towards the door with one of their upper hands. "We have nothing more to say to you at this time."

The Admiral nods and turns to go. She tosses Toreval a thoroughly pleased look as she walks away, patting Li briefly on the shoulder when she passes him. Li stays where he is. Thankfully, Toreval had remembered to explain to both humans that as their Navigator, he would need to wait until *they themself* were dismissed as well before departing.

The Eldest waits for a full minute after the Admiral has gone to speak again. "As for *you*, Celadon Toreval…"

"Yes, Eldest?" Toreval takes a step forward. They're not sure whether being addressed by their name rather than their title is a good sign.

"The Council has discussed *your* actions today at length." The Eldest flicks their ears lightly in the direction of the Elders sitting around them. "You have caused a great disturbance among us, using the Youngest's role as you have."

Toreval remains silent, keeping their calm, respectful posture and resisting the urge to interrupt and try to defend themself for the moment. There's something in the Eldest's tone that holds them back.

"In spite of the restrictions this Council normally places upon our members for their own safety and that of their kittens, our people's most dearly-held traditions, and our very nature as a species… *you* have declared that you will be leaving our Sanctuary to join Admiral Marvin's command and take part in this war the Novans are waging against our human friends." The Eldest fixes them with a piercing ancient gaze that still, somehow, seems to be colored with concern rather than disapproval.

Toreval dips their head respectfully in the silence that follows. "I have, Eldest, and I stand by what I have said. Even if no other Florivan follows me, I will go to aid our friends—and to protect our people and this Sanctuary with my life if need be."

"We are well aware of your dedication to your cause, Celadon Toreval." The Eldest taps their cane once on the floor to quiet a few stray murmurs from the upper balconies before they continue to speak. "After a lengthy deliberation... and in consideration of your personal circumstances... we find no reason to deny *your* choice either. Nor will we be officially relieving you of your title and ceremonial role as an Elder and the Youngest of this Council—*despite* the legally exiled status you are forcing us to place upon you in order to make it clear to any who might question that your actions are your own and neither the will of this Council nor our people. When you leave with Admiral Marvin, it is the will of this Council that you will not return here until your involvement in the war is at an end. Do you understand, Youngest?"

"I understand, Eldest." Toreval dips their head respectfully once more. "And I thank you and the rest of the Elders gathered here for allowing this." Somehow, despite the passing thought that they might be the first ever to be thrown out of the Council altogether, Toreval hasn't had time to consider that the other Elders might feel the need to prevent them from leaving. A new wave of relief is washing over them, although one tinged with a regret that they cannot name.

"You will, however," the Eldest continues, "be the *only* Elder permitted to take this path. The Council is agreed that the prospective danger is too far great to allow any other Elder or destined Elder to follow you. If others among our people volunteer to join you in serving the Admiral, they will be joining you in your exiled status as well and placing themselves into your house and your line for as long as they serve. We expect you to care for them as you would your own."

"Of course, Eldest."

"Do *not* make us regret this decision, Celadon Toreval."

"I won't, Eldest." Toreval makes a small bow to the Eldest and the rest of the Council, hands once again in a posture of gratitude. They understand the request underneath the Eldest's words well enough; they cannot be asked openly due to the Council's decision, but it will fall to *them* to act as liaison between the Council and the Fleet. They will have to remember to explain the nuance of all of this to the Admiral later.

"Now..." The Eldest stretches out their upper right hand and makes a beckoning motion. "Step forward, Ensign Hsu Li of the Sol Coalition Defense Fleet. We would have words with you."

Toreval catches a glimpse of that same confused expression Li wore earlier as he comes to stand by their side. If they'd known the Eldest would have anything to say to him, they'd have given a warning—but this move is unexpected even to them.

"Yes, Eldest?" Li asks, doing his best to imitate Toreval's respectful folded-hands posture.

Toreval is immediately grateful that Li has been quick to pick up on Council protocols. Whatever the Eldest wants with him, they know it will go more smoothly with him being polite.

"We understand that *you* have made the Navigator's compact with our Youngest, Celadon Toreval." The Eldest lightly taps the ground with their cane, fixing Li with that same piercingly formal gaze they turned on Toreval while pronouncing the Council's decision. "Is this true?"

"I have, Eldest, yes."

"There are those among this Council who wonder if it was your Admiral's *intent* by bringing you here to lure one of our Elders into her service in order to influence the decisions we have made."

"I assure you it was not, Eldest."

"And yet here you are," says Toreval's parent dryly, cutting into the conversation, "having come as a mere *assistant*, but leaving with the Youngest of this Council at your side."

Li glances to Toreval briefly before he replies. Toreval wishes they could think of something to help him, but in this instance they know there is nothing they could say which would improve the situation. They try to give him a reassuring expression in return anyway.

"Whatever the Admiral's plans might have been, Elder Lazurite, I assure you, I did not seek anyone out under her orders." Li's voice takes on a uniquely calm and charming tone that Toreval is sure they've never heard him use before. His whole demeanor, in fact, has shifted to match—so much of a difference from the confusion and hesitation of only moments before that it catches them by surprise.

"Is that so?" Toreval's parent raises an eyebrow suspiciously.

"It is, yes." Li's voice and body language remain all bright confidence and honeyed charm. "Elder Celadon and I became friends by chance while I was enjoying the hospitality of your planet. They didn't even tell me they were on the Council until a few days ago."

Toreval is quite impressed by how quickly Li comes to this response—it's true, of course, but it leaves out enough of their *own* maneuverings and his intuition about their identity so as to seem perfectly innocent.

"We can accept this answer, young Navigator." The Eldest waves a hand in the direction of Toreval's parent before the interrogation can continue. "It is not our intention to put you on trial."

"Thank you, Eldest." Li dips his head politely. "I understand this is something of an unusual situation. Please believe me when I say that I am *honored* to be Elder Celadon's Navigator, and I will be doing everything in my power to keep them safe while we're with the Fleet—and after, if they decide they'd like to be a civilian again when the war ends."

When he glances back to Toreval this time, Li has a smile on that they take to mean he's serious about that. They can't help smiling back, still amazed at how well he's taken the situation they've put him in. They're beginning to let themself look forward to sharing their life with him—although they know they still have a *lot* of things to discuss and explain before the two of them leave Procyon.

"Do you understand, then, Navigator Hsu Li," the Eldest asks slowly, looking at Li with an ancient calmness and curiosity of their own, "the *magnitude* of the responsibility you have assumed?"

"I believe that I do, Eldest, yes."

"We hope that you do, young Navigator. Our Youngest here is reckless... troublesome... *impulsive*... you may have noticed this?" The Eldest sounds almost *amused* as they say this.

Li seems to be holding back a chuckle himself when he responds. "I have, Eldest—but that's part of why we've become friends, I think. I needed a bit less caution in my life."

Toreval has a feeling that he's specifically thinking of when he almost fell on the way down from the rock spire—this statement is almost word-for-word what they said when they caught him.

"You may find you've taken on more excitement than you bargained for, young Navigator." The Eldest gives Toreval a knowing look and then returns their attention fully to Li. "In any case, it remains that you have accepted a named Elder of this Council for your counterpart. It is *unprecedented* in the history of our people's friendship with yours for such a thing to take place... as usually it is *understood* by our Elders where their duties and loyalties must lie."

"So I've been told, Eldest."

"Because of this... we must take an *equally* unprecedented step with you." The Eldest stands and gestures pointedly to Li with their cane. "Come here, Navigator Hsu Li."

Li glances back to Toreval again briefly before doing as the Eldest asks.

All they can do is offer him a sympathetic look and a bit of an equally brief shrug. Toreval doesn't know what to expect any more than he does, now. They knew there would be consequences for their actions, but they never considered that the Council might impose any of those consequences on *him* instead.

The long white silks of the Eldest's robes flow behind them as they step forward, meeting Li halfway between the dais and their usual seat at the head of the room. The Eldest leans on their cane with their lower hands and reaches out towards him with their upper pair.

"Give me your hands, Navigator."

Li doesn't question, but simply sets his tawny-pale alien hands into the deep grey-blue ones the Eldest is offering him.

Toreval only hopes he doesn't come to regret whatever is about to happen.

"The Youngest of this Council has chosen you for their Navigator and counterpart, Hsu Li," says the Eldest, "and we are prepared to give them into your care."

"Thank you, Eldest."

"Be silent, now, save to answer my questions... and keep your eyes *closed*. Do you understand?"

"I do, Eldest, yes."

"Good. Now listen to me, young Navigator." The Eldest shifts the tone of their voice back to the slow, methodical mode they use for ritual pronouncements. "Like all those who bear the burden of the Elder, your counterpart is a rarity among our kind... more precious than you may yet understand."

Looking around them, Toreval sees all the eyes of the other Elders now fixed upon their Navigator and the Eldest. Even their parent has turned to watch intently, although still with a disapproving look on their face.

The Eldest raises one of their lower hands from their cane to gesture around the Council hall. "We are the children of the Strange. Our kind walks... where yours cannot."

This reminds Toreval entirely too much of the ceremonies they went through themself when they were named an Elder—but that *can't* be what the Eldest is doing. Li is *human*. It isn't safe.

"Our ways... our nature... everything that we are flows from there, even as you have seen us." The Eldest's eyes close, first the lower two, and then after a pointed look in Toreval's direction, the third.

Toreval feels the Eldest begin flickering even before they see it. A long moment passes, and the rapid, rhythmic shifting of light and *presence* over the Eldest's body passes over the young human's as well.

"We cannot be without it... for the Strange is within us."

Toreval couldn't stop what's happening now, even though they deeply want to.

Li can't possibly understand the danger he's in. There's no way Toreval could have prepared him for this. They don't want to see him hurt, but they can't do anything to protect him now. They don't dare interrupt—to break the Eldest's concentration would only put Li at greater risk.

They only hope he can hold fast against the influence of the Strange.

A long, silky silence fills the room for what feels like an age as Toreval stands there, helplessly watching the Eldest pull Li deeper into the fringes of the Strange and further out of the Normal. They can't remember how long a human could be expected to survive exposure to even a small amount of miasma without permanent damage. A long list of terrifying possibilities won't stop running through the back of their mind.

"The burdens of the Elder will weigh even more heavily away from this Sanctuary of our people. Are you prepared, young Navigator..." asks the Eldest, pausing for a long moment in the middle of the question, "...to help your counterpart bear them?"

"...I am, Eldest, yes." Li's voice is uncharacteristically distant and dreamlike. Toreval hopes that's not a sign of injury already being done to his mind.

"We would charge you... with the life of Celadon Toreval... with their safety... and with the lives that may come into your care through them. Will you accept this duty, young Navigator?"

"...I will, Eldest... yes."

Beyond the worrying distant quality in it, Li's voice almost seems to *shine* now as he speaks from the fringes of the veil which separates the Strange from the Normal. In Toreval's perception, through the flickering, even his entire being is brighter. Little Myrval is right, it seems— their friend is a Beacon by nature, and now, with what the Eldest is doing to him, he'll be one fully awakened. Toreval hopes that the resilience of such humans is, in truth, as great as the stories they've heard all their life would suggest. It may be Li's only hope of coming out of this unharmed.

"Do you understand, young Navigator... that by accepting all of this, your duty now will be to our people as well as to your own?"

"...I do, Eldest... and... I accept."

Watching helplessly from mere steps away, Toreval wonders if he'll even be able to *remember* any of this.

"Then in return... this Council accepts you as the counterpart of our Youngest... and as one who can be entrusted with the lives and future of our people." The Eldest pauses for a long moment, then lightly presses their own forehead to Li's. "And of my *own* accord, Hsu Li, I mark you now too before all who stand here in witness as a member of my line and household, that any Florivan who meets you may know that you are not only our people's chosen friend and guardian, but a true child of my heart."

"...Thank you... Eldest..."

The flickering slows over another long silence and then finally stops. The Eldest opens their eyes in sequence and sends a long, knowing look Toreval's way.

Toreval rushes forward.

The Eldest releases Li's hands just as Toreval reaches out to steady him with a well-placed lower arm against his mid-back. As Toreval sets the same side's upper arm behind his shoulders, they get close enough that they can hear his heart beating—and the rhythm is moving far too slowly for their liking. Li seems to barely be breathing at all. His eyes flutter open, and he remains standing, but his gaze is unfocused and distant.

"You may take your Navigator, now, Youngest... and depart with the Council's blessing on your compact with him." The Eldest nods to Toreval and moves back to their seat in a swish of white silks, barely seeming to cross the space between.

"Thank you, Eldest."

Toreval wastes no time in guiding Li out of the Council hall while he's still able to walk. If they didn't have so much else on their mind, they would be yelling curses at any Elder who thought this stunt was a good idea. If they ever find out whose idea it *was*, they will have some very choice words for them indeed.

They only hope Li comes out of this unharmed so they can properly apologize for what their impulsiveness has done to him.

In the end, Elder Caeruleus' Navigator, Joseph, and Elder Azul's Navigator, Rebecca, have to help Toreval half-carry Li back to their home—he's hardly in a state to walk as far as the guest lodgings on his own, especially since night has fallen while they were inside. Toreval is incredibly grateful to the two Navigators who'd been waiting in the hallway for their counterparts and offered their assistance, particularly considering that Li is more than a head taller than Toreval themself and they'd never have been able to properly carry him on their own if he'd passed out entirely.

For his part, although he's unsteady on his feet, Li manages to stay mostly upright and moving for the crossing of the southern courtyard. Given what's been done to him, Toreval is impressed he's anything resembling conscious at all.

The moment Toreval has him placed on the plush green couch in their sitting room, though, Li murmurs something that they don't understand and then leans over and falls asleep with his head resting on their folded legs. The full length of his leaf-black hair flows like a liquid along the amber silks of their robes.

"Well, I'll ask Cae later what happened to him," Joseph says, leaning against the archway leading to Toreval's kitchen, "but at least we got him here before he passed out. Would you like me to go find Admiral Marvin for you? I think she mentioned she was off to send some relay messages when she passed us in the hall as she was leaving."

"I'd be grateful if you did." Toreval holds back a sigh. "And if it's not too much trouble, would you mind dropping by Indigo and Monica's too and telling Lapis where I am? Jade won't be home from their work with the other Star-Keepers until well past dark, and I don't want Lapis to be out so late waiting for the two of us to come get them..."

"Of course." Joseph nods and turns to go. "I hope your young friend here is okay."

"So do I."

Toreval looks down at Li's surprisingly peaceful face for a long moment in silence. They couldn't even begin to describe how concerned they are for him, but once again, all they can do is *wait*.

"So, Donnie. This is your Navigator, then?" Rebecca asks, perching on the armrest of the couch beside Toreval now. This deep brown human with tightly wound grey curls is one of Toreval's oldest friends and every bit the mentor to them that Elder Azul is. They owe her their life, in many ways, too. Needless to say, Toreval's incredibly glad she was there to help them when they came out of the Council Hall.

"He is, yes." Toreval can't help smiling as they say this. It's the first time they've truly been able to say that, now that their compact with him has been properly declared, and as worried as they are for Li, it's a surprisingly pleasing feeling to be able to claim their human friend openly as their counterpart.

"Hmm." Rebecca looks over at Li curiously. "Young. Capable?"

"I think he will be."

Rebecca falls silent for a moment, seeming to consider this, then lightly sets a hand on Toreval's shoulder. "You know, 'Zul and I always thought you'd have been better off if you'd taken a counterpart before?"

"Oh, did you?"

"Hmm. Yes. It would have been good to keep you out in the stars where you belong."

Toreval turns their third eye to her pointedly. "You *know* why I couldn't."

"Yeah, I remember."

A silence falls on the room for several minutes, save for the slow, gentle sound of Li's breathing. There are things among old friends that don't need to be said aloud to be understood. The circumstances surrounding Toreval's abruptly-ended apprenticeship are one of them.

Toreval can feel a bit of warmth coming back to Li's body now. He's felt unnaturally cold from the moment they caught him in the Council Hall, but now that seems to be wearing off. They can feel the edges of dreams shining off of him, too, now. Beacon that he is, those aren't hard even for someone as inexperienced with the nuances of interacting with them as Toreval to sense. It's an encouraging set of signs.

After a while longer sitting in companionable silence, Rebecca stands to go.

"Well... I'd better head back before 'Zul starts wondering where I've gone. You'll have to let us know when he's recovered so we can properly meet him."

"Thank you, Rebecca. I will."

"For what it's worth, Donnie?" Rebecca pauses beside Toreval as she leaves, setting a reassuringly warm hand on their shoulder once more. "I don't think it's so odd now that none of the prospects the Rangers offered clicked for you back when you were allowed to look."

"Oh?" Toreval tilts their head to one side. They weren't expecting such a statement, and they're not sure what to think of it.

"Hmm. No. I'd almost say you were waiting for *him*." Rebecca lets out a small chuckle, and then she departs.

As always, the old Navigator leaves Toreval with more to think about than they had to start with. Rebecca has that way about her—perhaps *she's* the one who taught them to be cryptic.

Toreval shifts carefully so they can reach over and pull the soft wave-patterned blanket from its resting place at the back of the couch down and drape it over their sleeping Navigator. Li doesn't stir at all when they settle back into a comfortable position and start unpinning their headdress.

All they can do now is sit and watch over him.

Toreval has no idea what they're going to say when he wakes up.

When Joseph finally returns with Admiral Marvin almost half an hour later, she is quite understandably *alarmed* by her assistant's condition. She'd been at the Interstellar Communications building getting in contact with her people ever since she left the Council Hall, since they agreed beforehand that Toreval would need some time when everything was over to discuss things with their Navigator and introduce him properly to the rest of their small family. Needless to say, the present situation is *far* from what she would have expected to come back to.

Once she's alone in the room with them, the Admiral pulls one of the padded wooden stools from the other side of the sitting area over closer to the couch and sits. She looks between Toreval and Li for a few moments before crossing her arms over her chest and letting out a somewhat exasperatedly concerned breath.

"So, Youngest... *What* exactly happened after I left?"

Toreval hesitates. "It's... somewhat difficult to explain."

"Try."

"I suppose the best way to put it... is that the Council decided that they had to put Li through a version of the Elder's initiation in order to accept him as my Navigator. I wasn't informed until it was too late to warn him or stop it from happening." Toreval looks down to Li. He's still sleeping peacefully, and his heartbeat and breathing sound *far* more normal for a human. They're relieved that he at least seems to be recovering.

The Admiral pinches the bridge of her nose for a moment before looking back to Toreval with raised eyebrows. "Do I *want* to know what this initiation of yours entails?"

"Probably not."

"Tell me anyway."

"The ritual is mainly about answering questions that amount to a set of oaths we're expected to hold to. In Li's case..." Toreval lets out a small sigh. They've been trying to find the best way to tell her what happened ever since Rebecca left them, but it's still *awkward*, to say the least. Taking a page from Li's book, they decide it's probably best to just be blunt about it. "I suppose the simplest way to put it is that the Eldest took him halfway into the Strange so they could judge his character."

"Judge his—*How*?"

Toreval understands the Admiral's shock. There are a lot of things their people are not particularly open about with their human friends, especially when it comes to the nature of the Strange and their own abilities. In general, even *Navigators* are only ever told the details as a need arises for them to know. They know they'll have to explain at least some of those things to the Admiral eventually, of course, if she's going to be leading a fleet equipped with the Drive—although not *nearly* as many things as they will have to explain to Li.

"Suffice it to say that the Eldest has lived long enough to develop abilities that go *far* beyond those of the average Florivan, Admiral. They don't need the assistance of technology to step across the veil, nor to take someone with them." While true, this is not the *full* truth—but

Toreval is drained enough from the day's events themself that they don't want to go into details right now.

"I see..." The Admiral fixes them with a somewhat disbelieving stare. "I've *never* heard of such a thing being possible."

"It's not widely known."

The Admiral shakes her head. "I'm sure we'll discuss *that* another time. What about Ensign Hsu? How long was he exposed?"

"From my perspective? Eight, maybe ten minutes. It could have been far longer than that from his."

"I see." The Admiral pauses for a moment and raises an eyebrow. "Forgive me for asking this, Youngest... but you're *sure* they weren't trying to kill him?"

"They weren't," Toreval says simply, almost amused by the question. "It's not our way."

"I hope you're right about that." The Admiral sighs and raises a hand to rub at her temple for a moment as if staving off a headache. "How bad do you think he has it, then?"

"Li handled the ordeal a lot better than you'd expect, actually." Toreval brushes a lock of hair back out of their sleeping friend's face. "He just seems physically exhausted, more than anything. Compared to what could have happened, I'd say his reaction has been *incredibly* mild."

"I've seen a man go *mad* from a minor leak in a cargo freighter's Drive bay seals, years ago—it was horrifying to watch. You're telling me that Ensign Hsu here got himself pulled halfway in... and you think he just needs to sleep it off?" The Admiral's incredulous stare is even more piercing than the Eldest's was when they were addressing Toreval in the Council Hall.

"I won't be able to tell for sure until he wakes up whether there's lasting damage, but his dreams are calm. That's a good sign."

"I'll make arrangements to have a human medic look him over once he's awake, regardless." The Admiral crosses her arms over her chest once more and lightly shakes her head. "I'm sure one of the ships in orbit has one I could borrow for a few hours."

"Probably a good idea." Toreval nods in agreement. "Dr. Boyle with LSS *Caleana Major* is an old friend of mine—you shouldn't have any problems contacting him, since Elder Azul and Rebecca are still planet-side. He has more experience than most human doctors with things like this."

"I'll do that. You're keeping the Ensign here tonight?"

"He's my Navigator."

"I thought as much." The Admiral stands and readjusts her dark green uniform jacket. "Send for me if his condition changes."

"You're welcome to stay, Admiral."

"Thank you, Youngest, but no. I have work to do before I sleep and it's better I do that back at the guest house where there aren't any distractions. Besides, it's been a long day for all of us—a bit of a stroll under the stars would do me a world of good."

Toreval can't exactly argue with any of that.

"I can understand that, Admiral... and please, my name is Celadon. I've pledged myself to your service; as my Captain, you don't have to use either of my titles."

"I'll keep that in mind, then." Admiral Marvin flashes them a tired but friendly smile. "And since you've thrown your lot in with mine now, you might as well call me Jenny. We'll talk about your service to the Fleet once this doctor friend of yours is done checking your Navigator over tomorrow." She gives them a little wave as she departs. "Pleasant dreams, Celadon."

"Likewise, Jenny." Toreval doesn't think to tell her as she leaves that Florivans don't experience dreams themselves—they understand the sentiment well enough to know not to bother correcting her.

It's well past midnight when Ilmi returns from their work with the other Story-Keepers. Taldee has already been home for some time, and long since gone to sleep in the family nest.

"Nida? I saw the light on, are you still up?" Ilmi calls as they arrive, "I need to talk to you about—" They halt in the doorway of the sitting room, staring in shock at Toreval and the sleeping human who's still stretched out on the couch with his head resting on Toreval's legs. "—What in the stars is *he* doing here?"

"I'm watching over him to make sure he recovers." Toreval pitches their voice just a bit quieter than usual so as not to potentially disturb Li or Taldee.

"Recovers from *what*?" Ilmi narrows their eyes, but matches Toreval's volume.

Toreval sighs, then tells their eldest kitten as calmly as they can what went on in the Council session and why their newly-compacted Navigator is resting in their home instead of his guest quarters. They don't want to admit it, but they haven't been looking forward to explaining all of what they've done. They *know* it's bound to upset Ilmi to hear it—and they aren't wrong.

"*Stars*, Nida." Ilmi is still staring with a mix of shock and near-horror when Toreval finally comes to the end of their explanation. "Have you lost your *mind*?"

"I assure you, Ilmi, I'm perfectly sane."

"*Really*? Because I'm not so sure you are!"

"Ilmi..."

Ilmi plops down onto the stool that's still sitting opposite Toreval with a huff so the two of them are eyes-to-eyes. They have all four of their icy greenish-blue arms crossed still, but lift one of the upper hands to gesture pointedly as they continue speaking. "*First* you insist I let Taldee keep playing at befriending these suspicious military humans, and *then* I find out that all the times I haven't been able to find you lately you've been out scampering all over the city with *this* one like a *kitten* and making all sorts of conspiracies with the Admiral he belongs to—all of which I *tried* to be reasonable about, since you told me you needed to get information from the two of them..."

"Which I *do* appreciate—"

"—But *now* you're telling me that he's your *Navigator* and you're *leaving* and the Council just—" Ilmi breaks off mid-sentence with a frustrated groan, glaring pointedly at the sleeping human.

Toreval sighs lightly. They were too caught up in the day's goings-on at first, but they've had ample time now to realize that Ilmi wouldn't react well to seeing a near-stranger in their home like this, even *without* the current circumstances. They're grateful at least that their older child is keeping the frustrations they're venting at a level whisper—not so much because they're afraid the conversation will wake Li, but more because Taldee is sleeping upstairs in the family nest and this *isn't* a conversation their youngest needs to be awakened by and overhear.

"It's not as dramatic as all that, Ilmi—"

"—Says the person who *jumped off a balcony* this afternoon?" Ilmi asks dryly, rolling their third eye.

"Ah." Toreval lets out a sheepish chuckle. They'd not thought to include that particular detail in their explanation of what went on in the Council session. "You've heard about that, then?"

"Elder Kyanite came in after the Council session to work with the rest of us." Ilmi fixes them with a pointedly disapproving stare. "Just before I left to come home, they mentioned they were concerned you might have injured yourself again, considering your condition—but *naturally* they wouldn't tell me anything *else* because tradition says I have to get my news from the head of the family even when *the head of my family is the one causing trouble.*"

"Ah." Toreval sighs softly. "Well... in any case, I *didn't* injure myself and my 'condition' has nothing to do with any of this—"

"—*Except* that it's why you're getting away with doing something as dangerously *stupid* as running away to join this 'Defense Fleet' nonsense."

Toreval falls silent for a moment. They can't deny that the Council took their medical history into account as reason enough to allow them to leave. They're painfully aware that Taldee is the last kitten they'll ever have, and how close to a gesture of pity their naming as an Elder was. Still, they'd rather not think about that aspect of their existence at the moment, much less discuss it.

"I *did* consult your opinion on all of this before I made my decision, Ilmi."

"Not that you actually *listened* to me about any of it." Ilmi pointedly looks away from them now, recrossing all four of their arms. The silver tuft at the end of their tail twitches angrily, making the little enameled bangles they wear on it jingle brightly. "Or seem to *care* about what I think, since you went and made your compact with this... this *stranger*... without even telling me you were considering taking a counterpart at all."

Toreval stays silent for a few moments, trying to find the right words to say.

They hadn't told Ilmi the full details of the time they've been spending with Li initially because they know how Ilmi feels about humans and didn't want to upset them. They somehow didn't consider that their impulsive decision to claim him as their counterpart this afternoon would be a more painful thing for their sweet eldest kitten to accept *because* of that secrecy.

"I'm sorry, Ilmi," Toreval says at last. "I'll admit that everything today has gone a bit more suddenly than I'd planned."

"But you *were* planning this, weren't you?" Ilmi glances back over at them with another agitated, jingling swish of their tail.

"Well... Only some parts of it," Toreval admits. "The rest has just sort of... happened as it's happened. If the Council hadn't forced my hands, I'm not sure if I'd have gone as far as I have."

"I *know* you, Nida," Ilmi says with a trace of a hiss. "You would have, somehow. This is what you've always wanted, isn't it? Some human or other to run away with?"

The words sting far deeper than Toreval would ever let themself acknowledge outright. There's a painful note of truth to it; one they didn't realize was still there, as they'd long ago thought they'd accepted their place in the world and the life that their own nature and their people's customs had dictated for them. They never recognized before now that Ilmi—sweet, sensitive, perceptive kitten that they are—would have noticed and *remembered* just how much Toreval had still been struggling to let go of their longing for a life of adventure among the stars when they and their littermates were young. The two of them have never spoken of that before now, not like this, but it's common knowledge that Toreval had thought they'd be walking a very different path when they first left Procyon, and they returned and *stayed* only because tradition and their parent agreed that they must.

Still, that's hardly the point at hand.

"I'm not running away, Ilmi—"

"—You're *leaving*. Like you let Iralee and Inayan leave—and if you'd just convinced them to stay *here* with *us* where it's *safe*..." Ilmi's voice catches on the words. Their ears droop as they fall silent and begin to absently straighten the fluff at the tip of their tail with their lower pair of hands.

"I know." Toreval sighs, breaking the silence. "You think I don't blame myself for encouraging the three of you to take advantage of the opportunities I never had? Or for letting your littermates do what they thought was right even though I *knew* there was a possibility they'd be in danger?"

"Then *why* are you doing this now?" Ilmi's voice falls softer, into a desperately pleading tone.

"Because they *were* right. And I have to see this through—for them, if not for all of us."

"And I'm supposed to accept that?"

"You don't have to, but it's the truth."

Ilmi looks away from them again, still seething with a pained frustration Toreval recognizes all too well. "Who even *is* this human that you're willing to abandon us for?"

"I'm not abandoning anyone," Toreval says plainly, wishing Ilmi had sat closer so they could reach and pull them into a hug right now. *They* need that reassurance almost as much as they're sure their kitten does. "I would *never* abandon my kittens. Not for all the stars."

"You're *leaving*." Ilmi repeats. "With him."

"You can come with us, Ilmi."

"And do what?" Ilmi hisses. "Let myself be *assigned* to one of your military humans and become a *tool* for this war of theirs that I want no part in?"

"You wouldn't be assigned to anyone. You'd be free to choose any Navigator you wanted, same as ever—"

"—I don't *want* anyone! You *know* that!"

Toreval recognizes the tone in Ilmi's voice all too well. It resonates so deeply in their own soul that it's painful.

"Ilmi," Toreval says, trying to be comforting, "you know I'd never force you to take one at all. But if you'd come with me—"

"—All I've ever wanted in the world is to be *here* with my *family*! You already let these humans take my littermates away—why do you have to let them take *you* too?"

"No one's *taken* anyone away, Ilmi. I'm doing this because I want to keep you and all of our people safe—"

"—That's what Inayan and Iralee said, and look what happened to *them*!" For a moment, Ilmi seems on the edge of tears, but then their tone and bearing falls painfully firm and serious. "That Admiral person may have used this 'friend' of yours to brainwash you too, Nida, but I will *never* trust her—or anyone who works for her."

"I haven't been brainwashed, Ilmi." Toreval sighs softly. They expected Ilmi to be upset, but perhaps not to this extent. "My thoughts about the situation lined up with Admiral Marvin's, that's all."

"If it's *not* brainwashing, then something *else* has to be wrong with you! You're impulsive, Nida, but you're never this *stupid* about it." Ilmi shakes their head, still glowering at Li. "You've only known these humans for a month. That's not time enough to get to know anyone!"

Toreval finds themself having to force back an unexpected laugh. "You know, Ilmi, if you would just give Li a chance, I think you'd like him? He said the same thing when *he* realized he was the Navigator I'd told the Council I'd taken."

"When he—*What?*"

"I... *may* have come up with that idea on the spot," Toreval admits. "Li took to it well enough, for not having any warning, thankfully. I'm not sure what the Council would have done if he'd turned me down."

"*Nida*. You can't just—I—" Ilmi lets out another frustrated groan and stands up from their stool. "I can't listen to any more of this."

"Ilmi—"

"—I'll talk to you once you come to your senses, Nida." Ilmi waves one of their lower hands as they stalk towards the door. "But I don't want anything to do with this human of yours, and I *won't* share a nest with him."

"Ilmi..."

Ilmi pauses, setting both right hands on the arched door frame that leads to the kitchen and leaning on it for a long moment. When they speak, finally, only a single one of their ears swivels towards Toreval—the rest of their face remains fixed in place, looking pointedly away.

"I love you, Nida," they say, sadly, "but this is something I will *never* be able to accept."

Toreval watches their eldest kitten disappear into the night, unable to do anything more than hope that *someday* Ilmi will understand why they've done the things they have.

Sitting there in the darkness almost alone, Toreval's soul aches for the days when their kittens were small and never left their side. The only thing that keeps them from sinking into the despair that's been lurking in the back of their mind ever since the day they learned of Iralee and Inayan's fates is the warmth of their Navigator still silently sleeping with his head on their lap.

They can't let themself lose focus now—not when they have someone to watch over.

★

A while later, Taldee reappears from the family nest, looking lost and sleepy.

"Nida? Where's Ilmi? I woke up and it was *cold* and I was still alone…"

"Oh, sweetheart…" Toreval reaches down to ruffle their kitten's hair. "Your sibling's going to be staying with your Ai-Nida and entiles tonight, that's all."

Taldee looks up at them with wide, concerned eyes. "Is Ilmi still mad at you for letting me play with your human friends?"

Toreval sighs. "No, dear, I don't think that's what's on their mind anymore."

Luckily, Taldee is young enough and sleepy enough still that they don't question this answer. An adorable yawn interrupts whatever they might have said in response.

"Do you think you can go back to sleep now, Taldee?" Toreval asks, still running their hand over the base of their kitten's ears in the way they know is best for calming them of any worries they might have absorbed.

"…Our nest is still cold. Can I stay here with you and Hsu Li?"

"Of course." Toreval pats the couch on the side of them that's not occupied by their sleeping Navigator. "There's room enough over here for you too."

After a few moments, Taldee's gotten themself comfortably curled up beside Toreval and has their head resting near where Li's is.

"Nida?" Taldee asks softly, already beginning to let out a bit of their contented sleepy kitten-purr in response to the continued stroking of their hair and ears.

"Yes, Taldee?"

"Are you really keeping Hsu Li?"

Toreval smiles in spite of themself. "I am, yes. He's going to be my Navigator—that makes him family, for you."

"Good." Taldee yawns again and snuggles just a touch closer to them. "I like him."

"So do I."

And with that, Taldee also falls asleep, curiosity apparently sated in favor of warmth and the comfort of their parent's gentle touch.

Toreval sits there in the darkness with their Navigator on one side and Taldee on the other, strangely content even as part of them is aching from the greater rift that seems to be growing between them and their eldest kitten.

Toreval watches over their Navigator through the night and well into the next morning.

The edges of his dreams remain calm and indistinct, as far as Toreval can tell, so they feel no need to do more than keep watch in case that changes. They count themself fortunate that they can rest at least partly in meditation with the echoes of the distant stars; there's no way they could let themself actually sleep in this situation. More than that, there's so much on their mind that they doubt they *could* sleep even if they tried.

Toreval takes some solace from Taldee's presence and gentle purring. Their youngest has always been a deep sleeper, even for a kitten, once they've found a comfortable position. When dawn comes and the kitten wakes, they spend a few minutes quietly talking to Taldee about what taking a counterpart actually *means* before sending them off to spend the day with Marbree and Myrval. Toreval is glad their young almost-siblings are still visiting so that Taldee has someone to play with.

Taldee, for their part, is nothing but excited about this arrangement—and seems to have forgotten all about any worries they may have had the night before by the time they scamper off to find their cousins. Toreval knows they'll have to talk to both of their kittens about their pending departure soon, but for now they're content to continue watching over their Navigator in the relative peace of their home.

It's well into the middle of the day when Li finally stirs.

A small yawn, and then he reaches up and rubs at his eyes. He looks up at Toreval after a moment, still half-asleep, but with none of the vagueness that was there when the Eldest first released him.

"Celadon?"

"Good morning, Li." Toreval could not even begin to describe the relief they feel seeing him awaken.

"It's morning?"

"It is for another hour or so."

"And I'm...?"

"In my home. How do you feel?"

Li sits up slowly, then leans back against the far armrest.

Toreval shifts their own position slightly so they're facing him, taking the opportunity to stretch out their legs.

"To tell you the truth? Like I've been out walking at the bottom of an ocean with lead boots on, and then suddenly got pulled up into micro-g."

"That's…" Toreval trails off, not having any idea how to respond. Li's description isn't all that far from what actually happened to him, conceptually.

"The world's weirdest hangover, is what I mean—but more vertigo and less headache and general suffering."

"You're not in any pain, I hope?"

"Not that much… I've had worse, believe it or not." Li tilts his head slightly to one side, then immediately seems to regret the motion. "How did I get here, anyway?"

"You don't remember, then?"

"I remember being in the Council Hall… and I was answering questions or something… and that the Eldest has *incredibly* cold hands. But that's about it."

"You're sure that's all?"

Li rubs at his temples for a few moments, then looks back to them. "I feel like there was something about standing in a grain field full of butterflies and the smell of lightning? That was probably a dream, though."

"It may not have been. Not entirely, at any rate."

"*Please*, Celadon." Li closes his eyes and rubs at one side of his head again. "I can't handle cryptic right now. Just tell me what's going on."

Toreval knows Li well enough now to see this request as a good sign that his mind is working properly and hasn't been damaged.

"To 'lay it out on the table,' as you would say… the Eldest took you halfway into the Strange as part of a simplified version of the Elder's initiation ritual."

Li's eyes flash open and widen considerably. "That's…" He trails off mid-thought and then rubs at his temples again for a few moments. "Well, that explains the weird hangover, at least."

"You're fortunate not to have been permanently damaged by the experience. The fact that you're awake now to talk to me is testament to your resilience."

"Thanks. I'm... glad I'm not running about as a madman too." Li forces a small laugh and then takes on a serious sort of curiosity again. "But why would they try something like that? And how's it even *possible*?"

"The Admiral asked me the same questions last night, you know?"

"Of course she did." Li groans lightly. "She's not happy about this, is she?"

"No," Toreval admits. "Concerned, more than anything. You're getting a full medical examination this afternoon, by the way."

"Joy of joys." Li pauses to stretch briefly before reassuming his firmly anchored position against the armrest.

"More vertigo?" Toreval asks, when they notice the way his hand is clinging to the couch cushion beside him.

"Yeah... don't think I'm going to try standing just yet."

Somehow, Toreval isn't surprised.

Since Li's not going anywhere, they leave him for a few minutes while they go into the other room and make tea. It's a good excuse to possibly delay the explanations they know they owe him; that, and it gives them a chance to send word to Jenny that her assistant is awake.

When they return, two mugs of steaming liquid in hand, Li is still exactly as they left him.

Li takes his mug in both hands, as if afraid he'd drop it otherwise. He takes a hesitant sip, then looks at Toreval over the mug with one eyebrow raised. "You didn't answer the questions—don't think I wouldn't notice."

"I was about to."

"Go ahead, then, I'm listening. The room doesn't try to move as much when you're talking."

Toreval takes a sip from their own mug and then does their best to find the right words to explain. They've spent most of the night trying to think through everything they need to tell him, but they still aren't sure if he'll be able to understand.

"As for *why*," Toreval begins, "I wasn't told specifically. My understanding is that the Council wanted to test your character and make sure you were fully committed to being my Navigator. That, and they seem to have decided that the only way they'd allow me to go with you was if you made a good impression on the Eldest during the initiation."

"You think I did, then?"

"The Eldest gave their blessing and adopted you into their line—and you're alive and mostly unharmed, which is *certainly* going to make an impression on anyone who was still against my taking you for my Navigator and leaving the system."

"They could have stopped you?"

"They could have *tried*."

Li flashes them a hint of a smirk. "That's what I thought."

Toreval can tell that they're going to have a longer conversation about some of the details of that subject with him later, when he's not still feeling the after-effects of his dip into the Strange. They don't mind waiting; it's not something they're in a mood to think about anyway.

"What was your other question?"

"Hmm? Oh, right." Li takes a sip and then looks back at them pointedly. "How in the *hell* did the Eldest pull me into the Strange without any Drive tech in the room?"

Toreval can't help but be amused by his phrasing. This is the first time they've ever heard Li use strong language of any kind—it's almost endearing that he seemingly reserves it for things that are *important*.

"The answer I gave Admiral Marvin was that the Eldest is capable of a lot of things which go beyond the abilities of the average Florivan."

Li arches an eyebrow curiously. "I take it that's *not* the full answer?"

"No, it's... a partial truth at best, really," Toreval admits.

"Are you going to tell me the full version, then? Or is that one of your cryptic Elder's secrets?"

"You're my *Navigator*, Li. There's a lot of things you'll eventually be trusted with that we don't openly discuss."

"I see. And is this one of those things?"

"Somewhat."

"So?"

Toreval looks down into their tea for a few moments before answering.

"*Theoretically*," they say at last, "any one of us could develop the skills to do what the Eldest did to you. Flickering's not an uncommon thing, really; it's something we teach to our kittens, even, when they're old enough to learn to walk in the Strange on their own. But being able to *control* it to a point where one can consciously take another person in tow like that—and at the same time stay anchored to a specific spot in the Normal, being fully aware of both places at once?" Toreval shakes their head. "That takes *talent* and decades of practice."

"So... the tech isn't entirely necessary, then, is it?"

Toreval once again notes that Li is *incredibly* perceptive for a human. They somehow hadn't expected him to make that leap of understanding so quickly, especially given his current condition.

"Our technology *is* necessary for jumping like we do with the Drive; I doubt even the Eldest could move a whole ship on their own without it. And the tech we've spent the last century adapting for your ships is *definitely* needed, since humans are so sensitive to the effects of the Strange and its miasmas."

Li chuckles, then takes another sip of his tea. "I am *well* aware of those effects now, yes."

"But as an individual?" Toreval continues, gesturing with their lower hands. "One has to have an anchor to call back to, of course, or a Beacon to reach for, or it's easy to be swept away... but it's definitely possible to dip in unaided. I've done that myself before."

"That doesn't sound entirely safe, even for you."

Toreval hesitates. He's right, of course, but not for the reason he's probably thinking. They know all too well how dangerous it can be to go into the Strange alone.

"We train to be safe in it, Li," they tell him, not ready yet to go into too much detail about any of this. "It's as much a part of our lives as breathing."

"I see." Li nods briefly, although he seems to regret the motion afterwards. "So, out of curiosity... if the Eldest had let go of me?"

"You'd have fallen to one side or the other, and even though I have a clear imprint on you now, I doubt it's strong enough yet that I could have found you in time if you'd been dropped in the Strange entirely."

"Ah. Noted."

Toreval takes another slow sip from their tea, watching his expression. Li seems to be taking all of this rather well, considering the circumstances. It bodes well for their future working with him. "Does that answer all of your questions, Li?"

"Eh? Mostly." Li shrugs. "I'm sure I'll come up with some more for you once my head clears."

"Fair enough."

Li takes a few moments to slowly drink some more from his own mug before he speaks again. "Did the Admiral say anything about when we're leaving, then?"

"I had a message from her earlier this morning. We've got passage for the four of us confirmed as far as Teegarden's Star with LSS *Caleana Major*—that's the light cargo ship Elder Azul and their Navigator, Rebecca, crew. Their Captain is quite excited about the prospect of helping us—I did my apprenticeship under them, actually, a long time ago. Old friendships run deep. Captain Montgomery has said she'll gladly make room for any other volunteers who might decide to join us, too."

"Good." Li nods slowly. "It won't be as fast as the Ranger ship that brought us here, I'm sure, but at least we have someone willing to take us to the shipyards."

"Well, *Caleana*'s one of the faster cargo vessels, in her own right. I've not seen the ship since its last overhaul, but I've heard good things about the improvements that have been made since I last flew with them."

Li pauses, then gives Toreval another curious look. "You said four? Who's your first recruit?"

"No recruits as yet, I'm afraid," Toreval says with a sigh. "I'm bringing Lapis with me."

Li reacts in a similar way to how they expect that Ilmi will when they break the news—almost choking on his tea from the shock.

"*Lapis*? Aren't they a bit... well... *young* to be joining a military operation?"

"They won't be *joining* anything." Toreval shakes their head. "Lapis isn't quite old enough to be apprenticed yet, any more than they're old enough to be separated from me at all... but they *will* be by the time we have the Fleet Drive-adapted and operational—assuming any other volunteers join us—and I'd already planned to ask Elder Azul to be their mentor. Lapis will be safe training with them for the next three or four years at least."

Li half nods and takes another slow sip from his mug. "Sounds like you've got that all planned out, then. Have you told them yet?"

"Not yet," Toreval admits.

"Judging from what I've seen of your little lightning-ball and the number of questions they've asked me and the Admiral about *everything* to do with space travel? They'll be bouncing off the walls excited about it."

"True." Toreval sighs. "They're not the one whose reaction concerns me, though."

Li gives them a pointedly knowing look. "So you've *not* told Jade the plan either, then?"

"I..." Toreval hesitates, remembering everything that went on the day before. "I haven't had time yet, really. I was somewhat preoccupied last night..."

"Sorry about that."

"It's not entirely your fault. Jade won't be happy about it any more than they were last night when I tried to tell them about what went on in the Council, I'm sure..." Toreval's tail swishes sadly as the memory of *that* conversation flashes through their mind again. "They've made it clear they don't agree with me, or with my taking a counterpart at all... but I hope they'll come to understand what I'm doing in time." They sigh regretfully and shake their head, trying to clear the more painful thoughts back so they can focus.

"And the rest of your family?"

"I'll have plenty of time to talk to my siblings before we leave, if there's anything our parent hasn't already told them by then."

"It sounds like you don't really want to talk to them, though."

Toreval takes a few sips of their tea before deciding on a response. Li's caught them off-guard again by picking up on that. They're not looking forward to the series of conversations in question at all.

"After yesterday?" they say, finally, "I doubt some of my family will be interested in speaking to me for a very long time."

"What, because of what happened in the Council session, or because you're leaving at all?"

"Mm... both, to some extent." Toreval makes a vague gesture with one of their upper hands. "Do you remember the rather... shall we say *vocal*... Elder in the yellow robes who sat beside the Eldest?"

"The one that kept interrupting and calling you by your other name? Lazurite, right? Yes, I remember talking to them. Why?"

"*They're* my parent."

"Ah." Li nods sympathetically. "I did wonder if it was something like that... yeah, that explains everything."

Toreval looks down at their tea again. They still haven't processed a lot of the feelings from yesterday, particularly when it comes to their parent's remarks and tone. It's not something they want to think too closely about just yet.

Li seems to pick up on the need for a change of subject.

"So, when do we fly out?"

"Twelve days, if all goes to plan—which is good for our purposes. It gives me time to settle my affairs here, at least."

"And to see how many of your people you can talk into tagging along with us?" Li flashes them a brief wry smile.

"That too, yes," Toreval admits.

"How are you planning to do that when we've been told not to go out recruiting?"

"The news from a Council session travels more quickly than you'd expect. Word of what I've done will spread through the families as the Elders tell their households what went on—meaning anyone who *is* inclined to join us will know to seek me out."

"Cryptic *and* subtle. Nice touch."

"Thank you."

"Do you think it will work?"

Toreval hesitates for a moment, swirling the remaining liquid around in their mug. "I think it *has* to. The Council's decisions leave us very few other options than to just quietly put it out there that the opportunity to serve with the Defense Fleet exists."

"I get that." Li nods, swirling the tea in his cup absently as he speaks. "It'll probably be easier once you draw in the first dozen or so and we have a functional proof of concept."

"I hope you're right about that."

"I've met a lot of the Nav prospects the Admiral's been recruiting on the hope that we'd be successful here," Li tells them. "There's plenty of good folks there to choose from. I don't know how it normally works, but if word of mouth fails to attract your people... we could always try sending a few of those prospects at a time here on leave. Someone's bound to latch onto them if given a chance."

"Not a bad idea, that."

"Well, it worked for me, didn't it?" Li teases, "and *I'm* not even qualified for Nav."

"I suppose it did at that," Toreval chuckles. "But as I told you before, your letters don't matter to me as much as you seem to think they should. You're my Navigator now, Li. No assessment or classification you could have would change that for all the stars."

Li shakes his head in amusement. "You *really* haven't spent much time in human circles, have you, Celadon?"

"Not since I was an apprentice, no—but enough to understand why it's supposedly an issue, though." Toreval shrugs. "Your people can suggest their 'highly qualified' prospects to the others we recruit all they want, Li, but by the time we get to Teegarden and Azul and Rebecca have helped me train you, you'll outclass all of them."

"Do you really think that," Li asks, "or are you just being encouraging because you're stuck with me?"

"I *chose* to be stuck with you, Li, remember?"

"Cryptic."

"Always." Toreval smiles affectionately. "But I *do* think you'll be a good Navigator. Like you said, you're going in as a glorified map reader—but you're that because you memorize star charts without trying and can calculate hex point conversions in your head as well as any Florivan can. *And* you already seem to be picking up how to work in tandem with me. All of that's only going to make things easier for you going forward."

"I'll take your word for it, then."

"Besides," Toreval teases, taking another small sip from their tea, "the Strange seems to like you."

"If this is what it feels like when the Strange *likes* someone, I'd hate to see what happens to people it doesn't get along with."

"I'll try not to let you get that close to it again."

"Much appreciated."

"In any case... You're my Navigator, Li. I'm confident you'll be up to the task."

There's a bit of a wry humor in Li's expression as he lifts his mug towards them in a mock toast. "To being stuck together, then."

Toreval mimics his gesture and leans across the couch to lightly clink the two mugs together. "To being stuck together."

"A LL RIGHT, DONNIE, THAT'S THE LAST CRATE loaded and secured," the shuttle pilot calls from the small craft's open cargo bay, dusting off their red-gloved hands. "I'll be done with my systems checks in twenty minutes and our departure window's in thirty. Anyone planning to fly with us had *better* be aboard by then or they'll have to hitch a ride with another ship—and that includes you and that kid you're calling your Navigator, mind!"

"Understood, Mx. Carlyle, thank you!" Toreval calls back from their perch on the domed roof of the nearest cargo shed.

"Good! And try not to break anything coming down from there—I know you must be happy to have someone who plays along with you at being a squirrel, but gravity'll get the both of you sooner or later and I don't want anyone blaming me for bringing you up to the ship in pieces."

"We'll be careful, don't worry!" Toreval waves brightly as their old friend disappears back into the belly of the shuttle.

"Are they always like that?" Li asks, raising his eyebrows. He's sitting right beside Toreval on the roof, watching the suns rising over the trees.

"Oh, I'd say age has mellowed them out a bit." Toreval can't help grinning at him. "They used to be the junior crewman who was put in charge of keeping me out of trouble whenever *Caleana* was in port somewhere—I have a feeling they're glad that's *your* job now."

For their part, Toreval is still amused that the same endearing grouch of a pilot who dropped them off here so many years ago is now taking them back up into space once again—as if somehow everything in between was just another planetside excursion and not an entire era of their life.

"Remind me to ask them for pointers, then." Li shakes his head lightly as if trying to not laugh. "I'm sure I'll need all the help I can get."

"Oh, I'm sure you won't have to ask. If I know Mx. Carlyle—and the rest of the crew that's left from the old days, for that matter—they're going to find *every* opportunity they can to embarrass me by telling you stories about what a handful I was as an apprentice."

Li does laugh this time, lightly. "I'd almost say you're looking forward to that."

"In an odd sort of way, I am," Toreval admits, turning their eyes back towards the city and the growing light of dawn. "I've missed them all, you know? *Caleana*'s crew were a second family to me... and I had to leave them sooner than anyone expected. If things had turned out differently, I might have stayed with them for at least another two years."

"I can understand that, I think." Li pauses, leaning back on his elbows and looking up at the sky. "That's why you're leaving Lapis with them, eventually, isn't it?"

"Mostly. Their older siblings did their apprenticeship under Elder Azul as well."

"Is that so? Family tradition, then?"

Toreval hesitates. They're not really ready to explain the other details of why they've had to make sure that their kittens would be trained by the same people who watched over their own adolescence. It's not a conversation they want to have with him just yet—especially not today.

"...You could say that, yes," they say, finally, absently readjusting the tail end of one of the long, wide amber silk ribbons they're wearing braided in with their hair.

"You're fussing with your ribbons again, Celadon."

"Am I?"

"You are. Are they tied in too tight or something?" The tone of Li's voice tells them he's using this as an excuse to redirect the conversation. It's a much-appreciated quality of his, that he seems to always pick up on the right moments to do that.

"Oh, no," Toreval replies, folding all four hands back together in their lap. "I'm just getting used to them, that's all. Although I think Elder Azul's going to have to show me again how they keep the silks in place for the braids, because it *still* feels like I've done something wrong."

The spacefaring Elder's more casual custom of dress is still new to them, but it's far more practical than the full robes and headdresses that Toreval's spent more than a third of their life in. It's more suitable for the work they'll be doing, too, especially since they'll be fitted out with some variation of a Fleet officer's uniform soon to match their Navigator and the hairstyle won't clash with that nearly as much as their formal headdress would. Toreval still hasn't decided yet whether or not they'll be trading out their signature amber for Fleet colors in the ribbons once they get to Teegarden's Star as a gesture towards their self-imposed exile. Either way, the thing that matters is that any of their people can identify them as an Elder with a glance.

"Does it?" Li leans around them to have a look for himself. "Well, it looks all right to me, for what it's worth."

"Thank you. I probably just need more practice."

Li seems about to say something else, but a jovial voice calling up from the pathway below their perch interrupts.

"Always up in the highest place you can find, eh, Celadon?"

"Always!" Toreval laughs, leaning down to wave at the trio of figures who must have approached from the outskirts of the city while they were distracted by their ribbons: one cloud-blue adult wearing a white shawl over the typical charcoal-grey uniform of a civilian space service QSD Engineer flanked closely by two familiar adolescents in matching white casual tunics.

"Wouldn't have you any other way—but it does make it a bit hard to carry on a conversation!"

"Hang on a moment, Sky, we'll be right down!"

Luckily, it's hardly a far distance for Toreval to jump—and while Li is naturally a bit more cautious about heights and landings, they know it won't take him long to climb down the nearby access ladder and join them.

On the ground, they're met with a long overdue hug.

"It's good to see you again, Laryven," they whisper, clinging to their almost-littermate tightly for a few moments. It's been *years* since they had a chance to do that.

"Likewise, Toreval!" Laryven grins broadly. "I seem to have had good timing coming home."

"Yes…" Toreval gives them a teasing nudge. "If by 'good timing,' you mean you've arrived just as *I'm* leaving."

"So Nida said—you've been up to no end of mischief lately, to hear them tell it."

Toreval laughs sheepishly. "I doubt the Eldest actually called it 'mischief,' did they?"

"Oh, no, but you know Nida; they use every formally disapproving word in the galaxy to describe the trouble you get into, but the tone says 'my mischievous heart's-kitten is doing their best and I wish I could still get away with being a balcony-jumping troublemaker myself.'" Laryven's ear twitches with amusement.

"Is that actually a *tradition* with your Council, or something?" Li asks, coming to stand at Toreval's side. "It seemed like an easy way to break a leg, to me."

"Not so much a tradition as the fact that Celadon here and my parent *both* seem to think that the laws of physics don't apply to them if there's a theatrical point to be made." Laryven rolls their third eye, making a face that says they're holding in no end of giggles. "Although to be fair, in Nida's case that might actually be *true* to some extent by now." They offer a hand to Li, with a genuinely interested sort of a smile. "You must be the Navigator everyone's told me about, then?"

"I must be at that." Li accepts a brief handshake. "You're welcome to call me Li."

"I was going to ask if I could, little brother." Laryven chuckles. "You're family, now, after all."

"We are?" Li looks to Toreval.

"Li, this is Sky Laryven of the Eldest's line," Toreval says with a fond gesture. "We were kittens together."

"Indeed we were!" Laryven's tail makes a happy wave. "Celadon here was practically one of my littermates, even if they *are* three years younger than me and Stream—and managed to get the two of us into *all* sorts of trouble, more often than not."

"That last bit certainly sounds in character, from what everyone else has told me about them." Li looks to Toreval with the edge of a laugh sparkling in his dark eyes. "Nice to meet you, Sky—and nice to see you two again, Ocean, River," he adds, nodding down to the two adolescents who have been standing quietly beside Laryven the whole time, "but I thought you said all of your goodbyes when the Admiral and Lapis got on the shuttle yesterday?"

"We did!" says Marbree, ever the more outgoing of the two, "but *today* we're here to say goodbye to you and Celadon."

"And to Sky," little Myrval adds with a sad drooping of their ears as they look to their older sibling, "even though they *just* got home."

"Oh?" Toreval looks to Laryven as well, raising their third eyebrow curiously.

"Well, Deirdre and I had a long talk about it last night after Nida gave me the news." Each of Laryven's lower pair of hands settles affectionately on the head of one of their younger siblings for a few moments as they explain. "She's up in orbit getting our things transferred over from *Cetorhinus* now—assuming you're still taking volunteers? We were about ready to let someone else take a turn at being Aoi and Margaret's secondary pair and seek out a ship of our own anyway, you know?"

Toreval can't ignore the impulse to embrace their almost-littermate again.

"You're both more than welcome," they say, once they let go, "and I'm grateful to have you. That makes an even dozen volunteers, now."

"Glad to hear I'm not the only one. And you can call it a baker's dozen—Stream and Mirabel are meeting us at Teegarden."

"They are?" Toreval can't help the stunned expression that passes across their face. "But they just became *Inia*'s Primary team a few months ago..."

"From what they said when Nida and I talked to them last night, Captain Argus is volunteering his ship too—*Inia* is small enough to be a scout vessel as soon as he drops off any of the crew that's not interested in joining the Fleet at the nearest spaceport." Laryven takes both of Toreval's upper hands in theirs and gives them a light squeeze. "Tradition wouldn't let us join your household before, Celadon, and you always insisted that Stream and I belonged in the stars. Let us stand with you now to protect them?"

Toreval finds their eyes growing moist. They squeeze Laryven's hands back. "Thank you, Sky. Truly."

"Anytime, Celadon." Laryven smiles softly. "So! Any others coming as pairs?"

"Surprisingly, you're not actually the first bringing a counterpart with them."

"Oh?" Laryven tilts their head curiously. "Who was, then?"

"*Indigo Taivin*, of all people." Toreval stifles a laugh. "They were my second volunteer, even."

"Really?" Laryven laughs brightly. "And here I was talking about baker's dozens... and the baker's six steps ahead of me as usual. I never thought *they'd* come out of retirement."

"Neither did I, but they have. Elder Woad is one of our strongest supporters in the Council, though, which I'm sure had some effect on their decision..." Toreval shakes their head. "I'm glad to have Indigo and Monica with us for sure—they're far better suited to training our less experienced volunteers than I am."

"I can't think of anyone who'd be better to have on your side." Laryven pauses a moment to look around and then towards the shuttle. "I take it they and the rest of your volunteers have all gone up to *Caleana* already?"

Toreval nods. "All but one. Indigo and the rest all took the other shuttle up yesterday when Elder Azul and Rebecca went, but my *first* volunteer is waiting for us at Teegarden. "

"Who's your—wait, no, let me guess..." Laryven gives Toreval a knowing look as the realization dawns on them. "Navy?"

"Who else?" Toreval shakes their head. "They sent word to me the moment Elder Bughaw finished telling them what went on in the Council."

"Considering they *already* made a point of finding a loophole so they could work at the shipyards? I'm not surprised." Laryven grins at them. "Looks like all of Elder Azul's most notorious apprentices are going to be in one spot again, then."

"It does, doesn't it?" Toreval chuckles. "I have no doubt they're already doing their best to *tell* Admiral Marvin all of the embarrassing stories they have about us..."

"No doubt." Laryven flicks their ears curiously. "Why didn't you go up with the rest, then?"

"I just had some other things to wrap up..."

"Oh?"

Toreval hesitates. They did, of course, have arrangements to make and last-minute cargo to ensure was loaded onto the shuttle, but their primary reason for waiting to leave for so long was based on the hope that Ilmi would let them have a chance to say goodbye.

"Well." They say at last, running a hand through their ribbons again to make sure they haven't fallen out. "The Admiral wanted to give a chance for any last-minute volunteers like *you* to find me, just in case."

"Ah." Laryven's tone and expression make it clear they don't believe that this is Toreval's only reason. "Don't worry too much about the numbers. Word's spreading well enough, Celadon—I wouldn't be surprised if you get *another* dozen by the time the next ship leaves for Teegarden."

"I hope you're right." Toreval does their best not to punctuate the statement with a sigh. They're grateful really that so many of their people have already joined them, especially because at first they were certain they'd be going to the Fleet alone—but at the same time, they know they don't have *nearly* enough volunteers yet to fully staff the defense of *one* star system, let alone the eight they've sworn their life to help protect.

"Now, Ocean, River," says Laryven, looking down to each of their youngest siblings in turn. "I believe Nida gave the two of you a task here aside from seeing me off?"

"Yes!" Marbree excitedly bounces over closer to Li, with little Myrval somewhat less enthusiastically following them. "Nida also sent us to say goodbye to *you* for them!"

"Is that so?" Li asks, with a particularly charming curiosity in his tone.

"Yes! And they said to tell you not to forget that you're one of our *siblings* now, and that they'll be writing to you like they do to the rest of us who are out in the stars—and to give you this!" Marbree turns with a dramatic gesture to Myrval, who pulls a neatly folded bundle of white fabric from the small satchel they're wearing and holds it out to Li.

"Thank you?" Li shoots Toreval a brief questioning glance over the heads of the two kittens.

"It's your family clothes!" Marbree explains excitedly. "The tunic is for formal things and when you come back to visit—Nida made sure there aren't too many arm holes and everything. And then *we* picked out the scarf, since the Admiral told us you usually wear them all the time when we asked her what you'd like."

"Well, you picked well, then." Li still sounds a touch confused, but he seems to be taking this in stride well enough. "And do thank your parent for thinking of me."

"They're *your* Nida too, now, Li." Marbree giggles. Myrval nods in agreement.

"Right." Li makes a point of nodding to both kittens as he corrects himself. "Thank *our* parent for me, then."

Laryven lets out a light laugh. "I *may* have promised to take a picture for them of you and Deirdre and Mirabel together all dressed up like proper members of the family after we all get to Teegarden, by the way. I hope you don't mind, little brother. Nida has something of a *collection* of photos of all of us—adopted humans included."

"I don't mind." Li runs a gentle hand over the top layer of shimmer-embroidered white silks with a hint of a growing smile. "And I don't think I can rightly refuse a request from the Eldest, can I?"

"Not easily," Toreval tells him, "but I'd support you if you wanted to." They know that in this case he's making a joke, but it still feels important to say this out loud. Li's adapted amazingly well to all of the changes they've so rapidly brought into his life, but they're well aware that he's still not familiar enough with their culture to really know where the boundaries of tradition are—or what's actually *expected* of him as a human who's now legally a child of the Eldest's line.

"I'll keep that in mind." Li nods, still smiling in a way that tells Toreval he's actually deeply touched by the gesture his new family has made.

"Well, now that that's settled..." Laryven leans down and holds their arms open to their siblings. "You two had best finish saying your see-you-laters and head back before Nida and Entile Caeruleus start wondering if you've stowed away with us."

Marbree and Myrval accept the embrace gladly, then after reluctantly letting go of their sibling scamper over and give an equally enthusiastic hug to Toreval.

"Now, you two be good when you go back up to *Deinocheirus* next week," Toreval tells them, "and try not to get into too much trouble before we see each other again, okay?"

"Oh, *you're* one to talk about getting into trouble, Celadon," Laryven giggles.

"What can I say?" Toreval rolls their third eye at their almost-littermate. "I'm something of an *expert* on that subject."

"*We* don't get into trouble, Celadon," Marbree replies matter-of-fact-ly, tugging on one of Toreval's lower sleeves. "We have *adventures*."

"*Ocean* has adventures," little Myrval corrects, mimicking Toreval's eye-roll. "*I* just go with them so we don't get in trouble for real."

"Well, then, I'm glad the two of you have each other." Toreval affectionately ruffles each kitten's hair in turn. They're glad that at least some part of their extended family has come to see them off—they almost expected to be leaving without any notice at all, not that they'd ever admit to that.

After Toreval lets the two of them go, Marbree turns to Li and tilts their head curiously.

"We've never had a brother before. Do you do goodbye hugs too, Li?"

"I'm not particularly the 'hug' type most of the time," Li admits, although still in his most charmingly amused tone. "Would a goodbye handshake be acceptable for now?"

Marbree looks to Myrval, who gives something of a relieved nod.

"That works for us!" Marbree declares. Handshakes accomplished, the two youngsters share one last lengthy embrace with Laryven before they disappear back down the path to the city.

"Those two are growing up *entirely* too fast," Laryven comments.

"They are," Toreval agrees. "And just wait until you see Lapis—they're taller than River now, believe it or not."

"Really?" Laryven laughs brightly. "Not that it would take much there, but I could have *sworn* that kitten of yours was still small enough to ride on my shoulder the last time we came home."

"They *were*, Sky—but that was almost three years ago." Toreval shakes their head. "The way Lapis is going now, I wouldn't be surprised if they end up taller than me by the time they're done growing."

Laryven grins and sets a hand on Toreval's head playfully. "And I say again: not that it would take much. There's a *reason* you used to get mistaken for the survivor-smallest of our litter, you know."

Toreval is about to make an equally playful reply drawing on the fact that Laryven and their littermate are *known* for being taller than the average Florivan, just as the Eldest is, but a light tap of Li's hand on their arm interrupts.

"Looks like we have more company." He gestures to a group of familiar figures approaching from the city path. "Do you want me to go ask Mx. Carlyle to see if they can hold the shuttle a bit longer in case this takes a while?"

"I..." Toreval is slightly too stunned by the recognition of the group to immediately answer.

"I'll go tell them—*your* place is at Celadon's side, little brother." Laryven gives Toreval a reassuring pat on the shoulder as they turn towards the shuttle. "Don't worry, we won't leave without you. Promise."

"Thank you," Toreval whispers. They take a breath to center themself and then step forward to meet the group, forcing a confident brightness into their tone to cover up the other things they're feeling. "Nida. Good morning... I didn't think you'd come."

"Celadon Toreval," says their parent with an almost sad sigh, stepping towards them out of the small collection of Toreval's siblings. "I know we were never able to imprint on each other properly when you were a kitten, and in the years since you returned from your apprenticeship, I don't believe the two of us have agreed on *anything* more than twice... and I *still* don't agree with what you're doing *at all*, regardless of the fact that the rest of the Council has decided to let you get away with it." They shake their head lightly and come to stand directly in front of Toreval. "But do you *really* think I'm letting one of my kittens leave this planet without properly saying goodbye to them?"

"Even if it's the one who's 'going against everything the Council stands for,' Nida?" Toreval themself doesn't know why they ask this. They have too many conflicting feelings at the moment to be sure.

Their parent lets out an equally conflicted-sounding sigh. "*Especially* if it's the one I shouldn't have said that to."

"You had a point, I'm sure," Toreval admits.

"Even so."

A moment of awkward silence, and then Toreval's parent holds out their arms.

Toreval accepts the embrace, allowing themself to be wrapped up in the soft layers of yellow silks for the first time in longer than they care to remember. There's a familiar comfort to this—one they hadn't expected to feel, but that they're grateful for in more ways than one.

"I do love you, Nida," Toreval whispers, "and I'm sorry. For a lot of things."

"And I you, Toreval," their parent replies, lightly setting one of their upper hands on Toreval's head and ruffling their ears. "And likewise." After a moment, they sigh again and release Toreval from the hug. "But forgive me if I hope you're proven wrong about all this."

"If being wrong means all of you are safe, I'll be okay with that." Toreval lets out a sigh of their own. "But I have to see this through."

"I know." Toreval's parent shakes their head. "The day *you* stop being stubborn about things you've decided is the day the galaxy folds in half, I'm sure. Now, your siblings came with me to wish you well—you'd best see to that if you want to leave on time."

Toreval hesitates for a moment as they look over the group of familiar faces and then softly asks, "Ilmi didn't come with you?"

"I offered. They said you were already aware of anything they might have had to say."

"Ah. I see."

Their parent's eyes soften lightly. "That one takes after you more than you think, Toreval. I'm not sure you see it, but it's there. Rest assured, they'll be safe here with us until you're ready to give up this nonsense and come home."

Toreval chooses not to comment on their parent's choice of phrasing. "Thank you, Nida."

Out of the corner of their third eye while they're in the middle of exchanging hugs with the few siblings they haven't had a chance to speak to since the Council's decision was made, Toreval sees their parent turn to Li. They swivel one of their ears to pick up on the conversation.

"Ensign." Their parent's tone is dry and formal.

"Elder Lazurite." Li's voice is back to that same incredibly charming tone he used when he stood before the Council.

"Do *not* mistake my presence here for approval. Of *any* of this—or of *you*, Beacon or not."

"I'll be sure not to."

"If this wayward kitten of mine comes to *any* harm as a result of being talked into taking such an *inexperienced* counterpart..." Toreval's parent trails off, a particularly half-hissing tone of unspoken promise echoing in their voice.

"I can assure you, Elder Lazurite, no one talked *Celadon* into anything." They hear Li forcing back a chuckle as he says this. "But I *will* do my best to become as good of a Navigator as they deserve—you have my word on that."

"Hmm."

It's at this point that Toreval finishes saying farewell to their three youngest siblings, all of whom have barely begun to lose their kitten fur in patches around their upper shoulder-blades. They take the opportunity to return to rescue their Navigator from the awkwardly threatening conversation he's found himself in.

"Nida, I think I'd better hand these three over to you before they try to stow away. You know how kittens get." Toreval plucks one squirrel-sized silver fluff of a sibling off of each of their shoulders and the third from the top of their head and holds them out gently to their parent.

"I do at that." Their parent smiles and takes custody of the first two kittens. "Too curious for their own good, sometimes—although *most* of them grow out of it sooner or later."

The third kitten makes a leap out of Toreval's hand and abruptly lands on Li's shoulder, curiously patting at the end of his long leaf-black ponytail with their upper pair of hands.

"Shiny!" declares the kitten, looking up at Li with wide, excited eyes. They hug his neck, their fluffy silver tail waving happily.

"Um... nice to meet you," Li says, carefully attempting to remove his small admirer. "But I think it's time for me and Celadon to get going."

"*Shiny!*" The kitten resists Li's hands, batting at them with pointed swishes of their tail. "Mine!"

"No, sweetheart," says Toreval, reaching up and giving their littlest sibling a soft scratch behind their ears to encourage them to loosen their grip on Li. "This one's mine. You'll have to wait until you're older to find a nice human like Li for your Navigator."

The kitten turns their eyes to Toreval with a distinctively disappointed expression and a trilling squeak to match.

"Now, what was I just saying?" Toreval's parent makes a familiarly exasperated huff. "*Myrie*! Come back here, little one, leave the human alone."

Little Myrie looks back to their parent with a momentary pout before leaping off of Li's shoulder to join their littermates in the folds of their parent's yellow robes. After a moment, all three kittens wave to him and Toreval in unison. "Bye-bye Shiny! Bye-bye Tor'val!"

"We won't speak again until you return," Toreval's parent says, setting a hand on each kitten's head to quiet them down and prevent further escape attempts, "but please, do at least *try* to be careful, Toreval?"

"I will. Goodbye, Nida."

With that, Toreval turns and walks to the shuttle in silence, Li close beside them. A glance back through the small craft's rear viewport as they prepare for takeoff rewards them with a view of their parent and siblings still standing there, watching them leave.

Toreval's only regret in all of this, really, is that they aren't able to say goodbye to their eldest kitten. It hurts more than they expected, not knowing when they'll see Ilmi again, but they don't know any way they could have really done things differently. They've tried so many times since the night Ilmi left their home to contact them so the two of them could talk, but Ilmi has made it more than clear they aren't ready to do that.

"Are you okay?"

As the city below grows smaller and smaller and the shuttle nears the upper reaches of the planet's atmosphere, Toreval looks back from the viewport with a sigh. Once again, the bright, comforting warmth of their Navigator's voice has brought them back into the here and now.

"I will be."

"All right, then." Li's dark eyes still mark a touch of concern. After a few moments of silence, he gets a curious little sparkle in them instead. "Mind if I ask what's probably an *incredibly* stupid question, now that I'm thinking about it?"

"Go ahead. I could use the distraction." Toreval finds themself smiling, in spite of everything.

"I thought as much. So... the furry pocket-sized creature who jumped on my shoulder, there at the end. *They're* one of your siblings?"

"Myrie?" Toreval chuckles. This was hardly the top of the list of questions they'd expected he might ask. "Oh, yes. The youngest one, mind, along with their littermates— they're just about four years old. I'm not surprised they were curious about you. Nida doesn't exactly keep any humans around the house for them to meet."

"Ah. Okay, then." Li shakes his head lightly, sounding amused and a touch embarrassed. "I must have missed the briefing on what Florivan kittens were actually like, I guess. To tell you the truth, Celadon, I'd assumed all the other little fuzzy silver things I'd seen your fellow Elders carrying were some sort of... closely related domesticated species? Your sibling's the first one I've heard talking, at least..."

"...And our young are considerably different even from an older kitten like Lapis?"

"Yes. That exactly."

Toreval smiles. "No need to be embarrassed about the mistake, Li. That's one of the details about my species that's more... not secret, per se, more just... private?"

"Ah. Noted." Li nods. "They're cute, at least—amazing you all turn out human-sized, in the end, really."

"*I'd* say we're still cute as adults too," Laryven interjects with a laugh from where they're seated across the cabin aisle. "If a bit less soft and fuzzy and easy to lose in the Council house rafters and force someone to have to dismantle a section of the roof to retrieve them when their tail gets stuck..."

"Why does that sound like there's a story behind it?" Li asks, raising an eyebrow and looking between Toreval and Laryven.

"Oh, there *is*!" Laryven replies, gesturing grandly with both upper hands and their tail. "Want me to tell it to pass the time?"

"Sky!" Toreval can't hold the giggles in. "You're going to make him think I'm an accident waiting to happen, telling stories like that."

"But it's a good story! Besides—"

"—Would you kids *settle down* back there already!" calls Mx. Carlyle from the shuttle's cockpit. "I *swear* you two used to know how to pitch your voices so I could concentrate on flying without having to hear all of your chatter."

"Sorry, Mx. Carlyle!" Laryven and Toreval call back in unison, before both of them descend into somewhat quieter fits of giggling.

Once they have all the giggles out of their system, Toreval takes a deep breath and looks back to the viewport. Home is little more than the contours of the Long River now, seen from this distance as the planet continues to shrink beneath them.

"Feeling better?" Li asks.

"Hmm? Yes, actually. Thank you." Toreval smiles at him, a genuine one this time, and then looks back over to Laryven. "Both of you. I needed that."

The now-intentionally-quieter conversation on the rest of the flight up to dock with *Caleana Major* is centered around both some of the more notable adventures Toreval and Laryven went on as kittens and some more calm tales from Laryven's life as a working starship's jumper. Throughout it all, Toreval's eyes continue to wander towards the viewport and the ever-changing scene of the planet below.

They know whatever comes next won't be easy—far from it, if they're to be leading the Admiral's volunteers and running jumps through the Strange for her flagship.

At the same time, the planet below, all of their people who live there, the family they're leaving behind, their kittens: *these* are the things in their world that are worth protecting. Toreval can't see any way they could have made any different choices than they have.

They're ready, now, to face this new era of their life.

They have their Navigator at their side, too, as fine a friend as they could ever have hoped to find. He's young, for sure, and the two of them haven't known each other long, but Toreval knows already that Li will be there for them when they need him. They can't help being comforted by the idea of working with this bright young human and getting to know him better.

Somehow, sitting there in the shuttle listening to Laryven regale Li of one of their kittenhood misadventures, Toreval can't help but feel that whatever happens next, whatever consequences their actions might ultimately have, they'll be able to face it—because they know they won't have to face any of it alone.

★ The End ★

Appendix

Timeline of *Strange Space*™ Adventures

The following timeline lists all of the published *Strange Space*™ Adventures and Short Stories in roughly chronological order. Where stories feature major time skips, they have been placed based on the earliest events of that story.

Short Stories marked with *[1] can be found in *Tales of the Navigators: Volume 1*.

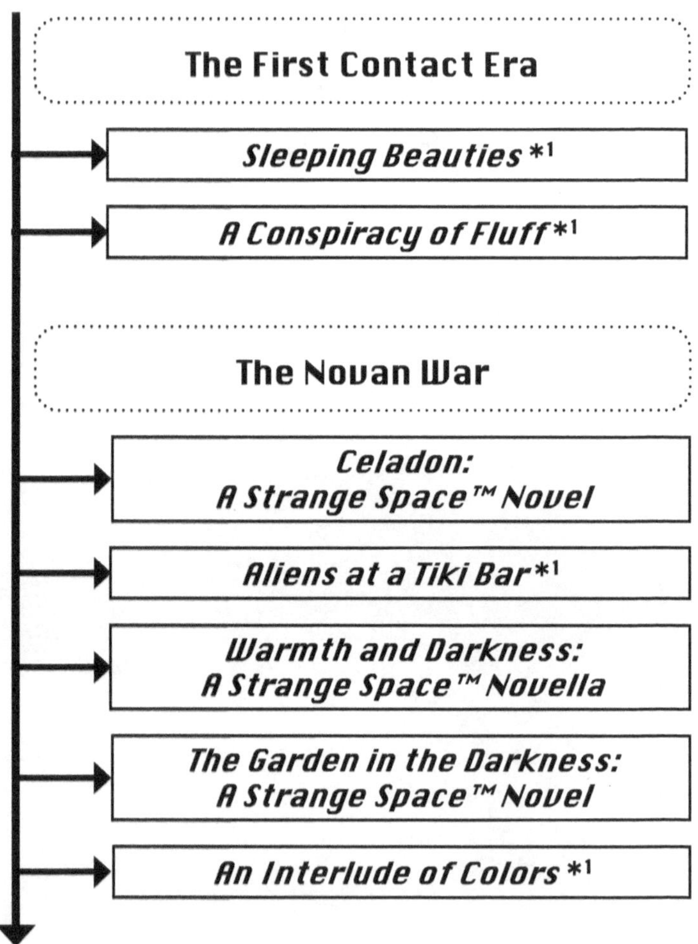

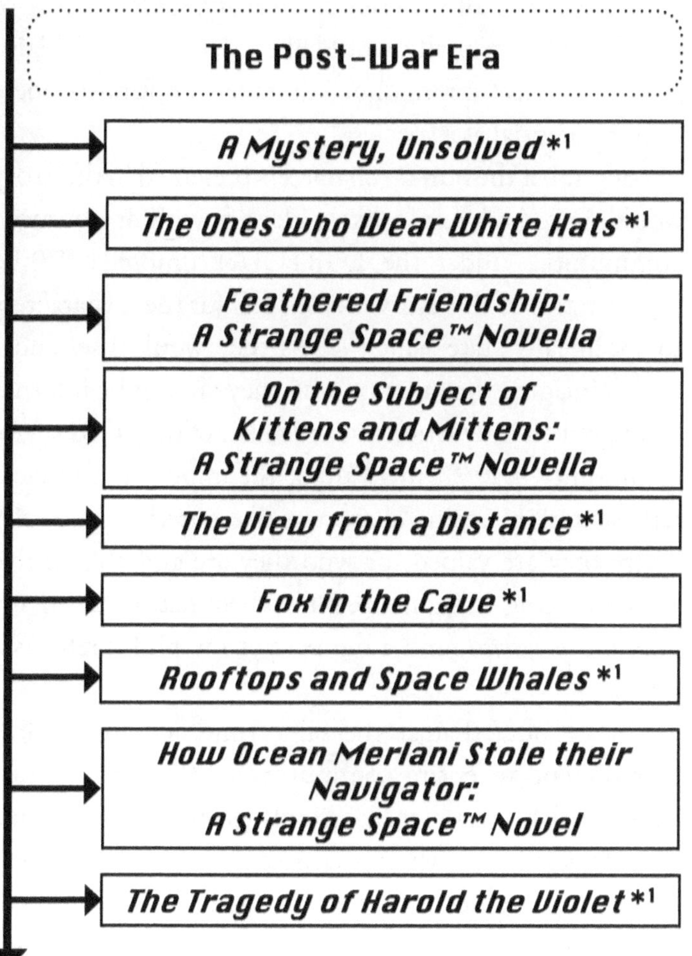

The Post-War Era
A Mystery, Unsolved *1
The Ones who Wear White Hats *1
Feathered Friendship:
A Strange Space™ Novella
On the Subject of
Kittens and Mittens:
A Strange Space™ Novella
The View from a Distance *1
Fox in the Cave *1
Rooftops and Space Whales *1
How Ocean Merlani Stole their
Navigator:
A Strange Space™ Novel
The Tragedy of Harold the Violet *1

On Character Identities and Pronouns

Celadon takes place in a far future setting in which human society has long since reached the stage of accepting and celebrating all varieties of diversity. This is a sort of world that I, personally, would like to live in. I don't claim it to be a *perfect* setting, but I do take an optimistic view of our potential as a species.

Several of the human characters presented in this story would, in today's terms, likely identify with one or more communities under the LGBTQIA+ umbrella. While the narrative of this story did not call for these characters to specifically state which labels they would use, and I like to imagine that a lot of who they are can be inferred through their interactions, as a member of the LGBTQIA+ community *myself*, I'm aware of the importance of clear representation. Seeing characters like ourselves in stories where they are valued for who they are and able to live without being marginalized for their nature is, in my opinion, *powerful*, and a big part of my philosophy as a writer.

Please note that at the same time, it is impossible to represent an entire community in the form of one character. My characters are simply themselves, and while they draw on my own experiences and those of people I know, they are not meant to be "perfect" renditions of one thing or another. Just like every human, their various identities are *aspects* of them, rather than the entirety of their personality.

That all being said, the following characters central to this story would like to "come out" to you and share this aspect of their lives:

Ensign Hsu Li would describe himself as pansexual and demi-romantic.

Admiral Jennifer Marvin would describe herself as aromantic and asexual.

On behalf of all of my characters, humans and Florivans alike, I'd like to thank you, dear reader, for being accepting of them and respecting their preferred sets of pronouns.

I hope that we all will one day live in a world like the one these characters inhabit, in which a person can openly be themself without fear. I do believe it's possible for us to get there, too; every small step we make in the right direction matters.

—Katie Silverwings

On Florivan Names

Florivan names consist of two parts: the 'public' name and the 'personal' name. The 'personal' or 'kitten-name' is given to a Florivan when they first open their eyes, while the 'public' name is chosen for them when they are old enough to be presented to the Council of Elders. Some kittens receive one or the other half of their name in honor of one of their ancestors or entiles, such as Celadon Toreval, whose personal name was given in memory of the noted healer Rain Toreval.

Personal names come from the ancestral Florivan language, and are largely untranslatable. All of the kittens in a litter will usually be given names with the same or similar initial sounds.

Public names are always words from human languages which connect somehow to the individual's coloring. Kittens, therefore, receive their public names once they have shed enough of their fur to show a large patch of a recognizable color. Elders will often carry a theme through the public names of their kittens such as different stones, plants, or a specific language of origin.

Florivans are most often addressed by their public names. Only Elders, family members, or the closest of friends will address or talk about a Florivan by their personal name, and then only in private. (Private, in this case, also extends to situations where only other Florivans or close friends of the family are present.)

Florivans also commonly take on nicknames which are used by their families, friends, and colleagues. Who can use a certain nickname for them depends on the situation and origin of the nickname. Celadon Toreval, for example, is occasionally called "Donnie" by the people who knew them as an adolescent, although usually only in private. Elders Caeruleus and Azul are called "Cae" and "'Zul" respectively only by their Navigators.

Florivan Elders are addressed formally with their title, although most of them will grant close friends and colleagues permission to address them by their public name alone outside of formal situations. The Eldest of the Council is a particular exception to this rule, as they are never referred to by name after assuming the role of Eldest, save by their siblings in private. Younger members of an Elder's line will call them 'Nida' ('Parent') or 'Ai-Nida' ('Grandparent') as appropriate in most situations. Apprentices to an Elder typically use their title as a sign of respect regardless of whose line they belong to, although the Elder may ask them to do otherwise in private.

On Florivan Biology and Culture

The Florivans are a curious species by nature.

Roughly humanoid in form with silver-striped blue skin, a second pair of arms below the first, a long tufted prehensile tail, catlike ears at the top of a head crowned with silver hair, and a third golden eye above the first two in the center of the forehead: it's easy to see them both as "human-like" and "entirely alien" all at once.

In the time of *Celadon*, the Florivans have been friends with humanity for just over a century. They've been working towards forming a fully integrated society with humanity ever since the exploration vessel LSS *Hulthemia* made first contact with scout ships from Procyon. Florivans had been serving on human starships as part of

Astral Navigator/Quantum Space Drive Engineer pairs almost from the beginning of the association between the two species.

Due to a series of devastating epidemics referred to as the "Jungle Plagues" and other events in their history as a species, at the time of Celadon, the total population of Florivans as a species is in the realm of two hundred thousand adults in total. The majority of these live in the Procyon star system on a planet known as the Sanctuary; roughly one thousand Florivans live at the human colony of Luyten's Star in an area called the North City Sanctuary, and another thousand or so currently serve with the crews of different starships, either as Quantum Space Drive Engineers or apprentices. Although the Jungle Plagues are mainly to blame for the current "endangered species" status of Florivans, their unusual biology is a core factor in their rarity and the slow rate at which their population can recover from any significant losses.

Florivans reproduce asexually, but only perhaps one in ten of them will ever undergo the metamorphosis to become a reproductive individual. Everything about the process is shrouded in secrecy, as far as humans are concerned. What *is* known, though, by the humans who find themselves as close friends with a Florivan with a reason to tell them, is that even the Florivans themselves cannot control or predict just *who* will undergo the metamorphosis or when it will happen to them.

It's also known that both the metamorphosis itself and the process of going physically into the Strange and "catching" a litter of kittens are potentially deadly. The families of reproductive individuals are very protective of them because of this, as is Florivan society as a whole. To that end, by the time of *Celadon*, a starship with a reproductive individual as one of its QSD Engineers will *always* have a second Nav/Quan team aboard.

Kittens are caught in litters of two to five, and start their lives as adorable silver-furred things about the size of a sugar glider. The Florivan parent carries their kittens in a pouch on their abdomen analogous to that of a kangaroo, although they aren't technically marsupials. The kittens grow to about the size of a red squirrel before they begin to mimic words and understand language. As kittens continue to grow, they shed their fur and reveal their unique shade of silver-striped blue skin. Around the same time they shed the last of their fur, Florivan kittens go through a series of growth spurts, after which they are similarly sized to human children and adolescents of the same age.

Occasionally, one kitten out of a litter will be smaller and develop more slowly than their littermates, having a more fragile constitution as a result. Referred to as "survivor-smallest", kittens, those who live long enough to open their eyes tend to take several additional years to grow to maturity. Although few such kittens prove strong enough to survive to adolescence, let alone adulthood, those who do are notable for their higher sensitivity and greater skills in working with Quantum Space. Notably, survivor-smallest kittens never undergo reproductive metamorphosis, but if they do reach adulthood, they are also known to live longer than the average Florivan by several decades.

Adolescent Florivans typically begin their apprenticeships to learn how to work in Quantum Space between the ages of ten and thirteen. The age at which a Florivan is released from their apprenticeship to either join the crew of another starship with their chosen human counterpart or seek additional training in their preferred career specialty depends entirely on the speed at which they mature into the skills their mentor is required to teach them in order to be safe and competent adults. Typically, Florivans are between fifteen and twenty when released from their apprenticeships. Florivans are considered 'adults' around the age of twenty to twenty-five, although they are usually fully grown and considered mature enough to select a human counterpart by age fifteen.

Usually, a Florivan reproductive individual is between thirty-five and fifty Earth-Standard years old at the time of their metamorphosis. On very rare occasions, a Florivan under the age of twenty-five will undergo the metamorphosis; these individuals seldom survive catching their first litter, and the younger they are the less likely it is they will survive the metamorphosis itself. Only one reproductive individual of this type, Celadon Toreval, has ever been known to survive an adolescent metamorphosis and live to be named an Elder of the Council.

Florivan culture, in many ways, has developed around these quirks of their biology. The leaders of Florivan society are the Elders of the Council: reproductive individuals who have survived both the metamorphosis and the catching of their first two litters of kittens. An Elder's littermates, traditionally, become part of their household to assist with their kittens. The Elder's "line" then grows with each of their subsequent litters, as well as other non-reproductive individuals who are adopted into the household over time.

Florivan society is built around family and close friendship, and has always been peaceful—in no small part because they instinctively consider all other members of their species as close kin. A Florivan's human counterpart is considered a member of their family as well, usually along the level of connection as a sibling. Florivan Elders commonly adopt the counterparts of their adult kittens into their households. Traditionally, the compacted Florivan/human pair is treated as a family unit, similar to what humans would call a platonic partnership. Such pairs typically form after the Florivan has finished their QSD Engineer apprenticeship and remain together for life.

Another important aspect of Florivan culture when compared with humanity is their relationship to the very human concepts of gender, sexuality, and romance. To put it bluntly, Florivans by nature have no concept of these things. They are, without exception, genderless, asexual, and aromantic, to use the most accurate human terms.

(Florivans do, of course, find the vast diversity among their human friends fascinating! It's part of why they think humans are neat.)

In light of their genderless nature, Florivans are always referred to with singular "they/them" personal pronouns in English and whatever neutral equivalent is most appropriate in other human languages. They also exclusively use neutral terms such as "Nida" (parent) and "Entile" (parent's sibling) when referring to other members of their family.

Katie Silverwings is an award-winning author, artist, and glassblower, originally from Texas and now a nomadic creative spirit. She holds a BA in English and History from McMurry University in Abilene, Texas, as well as a BA (Hons.) in Glass from the University for the Creative Arts in the UK. Silverwings identifies as aromantic, asexual, and genderfae; "she/her", "they/them", and "fae/faer" pronouns are all welcome.

Long fascinated by nature and space, Silverwings' speculative fiction work centers around notions of optimistic futurism, friendship, found family, and adventurous journeys into the known and unknown. Her characters do most of the driving, and she does her best to keep up and negotiate pleasing stories with them.

Silverwings' two cats are commonly found staring over her shoulder while she's writing. The small cloud of dark matter with eyes likes to sit in her lap and interfere with typing, while the calico makes operatic editorial comments from across the room.

www.KatieSilverwings.com

@KatieSilverwings

More Books
by Katie Silverwings

Warmth and Darkness

Admiral Jennifer Marvin used to think she'd seen everything the galaxy had to throw at her. That, though, was before she met the Florivan Elder Celadon Toreval. She can sum up this Quantum Space Drive Engineer and dear friend of hers in two words: *cryptic chaos*. Their preference for the company of the most troublesome humans they can possibly find in the Fleet's ranks doesn't make matters better.

These days, Admiral Marvin is just grateful that the galaxy occasionally sends her a sign that something unusual is about to upset her carefully laid plans. Whether she manages to see those signs in time to do anything about it, though, is always a gamble.

Join Admiral Marvin's crew aboard the starship SCV *Aegolius* as they face the next chapter in the tales of the Novan War, and find out what new adventure waits for them in the darkness.

Even in the depths of space, you can find warmth…

Available now from Amazon and Barnes & Noble and at
www.KatieSilverwings.com

The Garden in the Darkness

Feathered Friendship

How Ocean Merlani Stole their Navigator

Tales of the Navigators (Volume 1)

On the Subject of Kittens and Mittens